*NANCY DREW AND THE HARDY BOYS
TEAM UP
TO UNLOCK AN UNDERSEA SECRET!*

Nancy backflipped into the water, and swam behind Buck to the seaweed-festooned wreck of an old sailing vessel. In the murky water, the ship looked like the remains of an enormous sea monster.

With a human victim trapped in its belly— Buck! His head suddenly popped out from a porthole, bubbles streaming from his ripped air hose.

Nancy grabbed her spare mouthpiece. She slapped it to Buck's mouth and slowly pulled him to the surface. When they finally emerged, Nancy was angry. "That was a pretty dangerous stunt, Buck!" she said, shouting.

"No . . . ed . . . oddy . . ." he yelled back.

At least that's what it sounded like. "What?" Nancy asked.

"Dead body!" Buck replied, his voice straining. "I saw a dead body down there!"

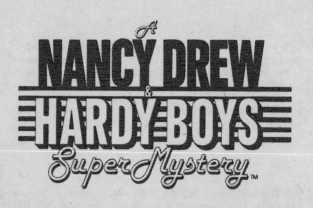

A NANCY DREW & HARDY BOYS Super Mystery™

SHOCK WAVES

Carolyn Keene

AN ARCHWAY PAPERBACK
Published by POCKET BOOKS
New York   London   Toronto   Sydney   Tokyo   Singapore

AN ARCHWAY PAPERBACK *Original*

An Archway Paperback published by
POCKET BOOKS, a division of Simon & Schuster Inc.
1230 Avenue of the Americas, New York, NY 10020

ISBN: 0-671-64919-1

First Archway Paperback printing April 1989

10 9 8 7 6 5 4 3

Printed in the U.S.A.

IL 7+

Chapter

One

SHOPPING? INDOORS? On a gorgeous day like this?" Nancy Drew's blue eyes sparkled as she took in the south Texas sky that was crystal clear, even at the airport. The hint of dark clouds on the horizon seemed light-years away. She picked up her luggage and threw it into the back of a red jeep.

"Why not?" said Nancy's friend Bess Marvin. "It's Monday morning. The stores will be empty."

"This is our vacation! We have only ten days, and I plan to *experience* Padre Island! Why don't we do something outdoors, like sailing or waterskiing or walking along miles of beaches—"

Next to her, a deeply tanned, dark-haired girl laughed. "Nancy the adventurer and outdoors girl! You know, you haven't changed one *bit* since summer camp!"

"How would *you* know, Mercedes?" Nancy said, an impish smile spreading across her face. Even though Nancy hadn't seen Mercedes Cole since camp three years earlier, she felt at ease with her. "I seem to recall you spent most of your time sneaking over to the boys' camp—"

"Nothing wrong with *that!*" came Bess's immediate reply.

Mercedes and her friends Kristin and Claire laughed. Leave it to Bess to put boy hunting into perspective, Nancy thought. To Bess, it was always open season!

With a shrug and a distracted toss of her long blond hair, Bess took a deep breath and valiantly tried to hoist an enormous suitcase into the Jeep. "I don't know *why* you two didn't let me get a skycap to help with this," she said to Nancy and her cousin, George Fayne.

George sighed. "Bess, you need a whole staff of people, not one skycap." She stepped toward Bess to help out.

As she moved, so did the other three girls—all at the same time. Nancy couldn't help but giggle. Five girls to lift one suitcase. One by one, the other girls joined Nancy until the whole group was paralyzed with laughter.

"Sorry," Bess murmured sheepishly after she brushed the tears of laughter from her eyes.

Claire touched Bess's arm sympathetically. "You pack like I do," she said with a Texas drawl. "An outfit for breakfast, something casual for walking around, two or three bathing suits, dressy clothes for the evening, a little old thing to lounge around in at night, and of course, some PJs." She cocked her head to one side, an innocent expression on her face. "And then I have to think about the *second* day!"

"Oh well," Mercedes said after the fresh burst of giggling died down. "I *was* going to take us all scuba diving, but it looks like we may be stopping off at the mall."

Nancy's head swung around at the sound of a car horn that bleated out the first few notes of a song.

"It's 'The Yellow Rose of Texas,'" Claire said in case the Yankees didn't recognize it.

Looking up the road, Mercedes shook her head. "Typical Buck Buchanan. Where on earth did he find *that* thing?"

Weaving toward them through the airport traffic was an old, funky white Oldsmobile convertible with faded psychedelic stripes. Nancy smiled at the sight of her old friends Frank and Joe Hardy whooping excitedly in the front seat. A month earlier Frank and Nancy had been talking on the phone about a case they had solved together. Nancy had casually mentioned her vacation, and Frank became interested in it for his and Joe's spring break.

Nancy was glad they had decided to come, but as usual, her feelings began tumbling whenever she looked at Frank. There was something about him, something in the intensity of his piercing brown eyes, his magnetic grin, his keen intelligence. . . .

Immediately Nancy felt herself blush—sitting behind the Hardys was her boyfriend, Ned Nickerson, who had gone along with the boys to the rental agency. She caught a glimpse of him as the old white car swung wide around a taxicab. As he flashed her that familiar, easy smile his soft dark eyes sent a message of love, and Nancy's emotions flipped once more—straight for Ned. She knew then that Frank Hardy could never put a dent in her feelings for Ned.

Another voice whooped a cowboy greeting from the back seat as the car slid to a stop at the curb beside them. Its engine coughed once and died.

A broad-shouldered blond guy leapt out of the

car, a movie-star grin of perfect white teeth gleaming against the deep bronze of his face. He leaned back in the car, pulled an oversize ten-gallon hat off the seat, put it on, and swept Mercedes backward with a huge kiss.

"Missed ya, honey," he said dramatically, with a thick Texas accent.

Mercedes giggled and pointed at the car. "Buck, I thought you guys went to the car-rental place, not the town dump!"

"Hey, we went to Rent-a-Jalopy," Buck protested. "Cheapest cars in town." He patted the hulking old convertible. "And the prettiest! I call her the White Bird!"

Buck's eyes impishly scanned each person— until he got to Nancy. His glance couldn't have rested more than a split-second longer on her, but there was a flicker in his expression that Nancy and the other girls couldn't miss. It was both a declaration and a promise—a declaration of interest, and a promise that he would be getting to know her on Padre Island.

Or was it just a habit of Buck's, a look he chose to bestow on one girl in every crowd? Mercedes had rhapsodized about Buck over the phone, and Nancy could tell that he lived up to his reputation: wild, charming, and attractive.

Attractive in a rough-and-rugged sense. Not

the strong, intelligent type that Nancy was drawn to—like Ned.

Or Frank.

"This thing is amazing!" Ned said, bounding toward Nancy.

"Okay, time to mobilize!" Buck called out. He walked over to the Jeep and reached for Bess's suitcase to toss in. "Let's pack these girls up so we can go scuba— Hey! What's in this thing? Bricks?"

As Buck struggled to lift the suitcase into the jeep, Bess's face turned beet red.

"Next time," she muttered to Nancy under her breath, "we pay a skycap!"

"I think the redhead is all right," Buck said as he ushered the Hardys and Ned into his beach house and flopped onto a white couch.

"Great place," Ned exclaimed, trying to ignore the remark. He took in the spacious living room, with its sisal rugs and wicker furniture. A huge, white-painted stone fireplace dominated one wall, and the other three were covered with posters of surfers, beach scenes, and sleek cars.

"Yeah, my mom and dad set it up for me," Buck replied matter-of-factly. "First time they visited they freaked out at the mess, and ever since then they hardly ever stop by. But they make sure someone comes in to clean once a week. Not bad, huh?"

"Not bad at all," Joe said, thinking of the chaos in his own room that he never had time to sort out.

Hopping up from the couch, Buck announced, "Tell you what. I'll take you guys up to your rooms—if you tell me about the redhead."

"Nancy?" Joe said, following Buck up the spiral staircase. He cast an uneasy glance over his shoulder at Ned. "Well, she goes with Ned. . . ."

"Whoa. Sorry," Buck shot back. He led them down a short corridor, at the end of which were two doors. "Didn't mean to butt in. I didn't know—"

Ned smiled and waved him off. "That's okay," he said good-naturedly.

"Besides," Joe said, "what about Mercedes? It looks like you and she are pretty tight."

Buck shrugged. "Yeah, Mercedes is great, but, hey—the field is big. Especially around this time of the year down here. I'm talking about girls from New England to L.A. You can learn about the whole country without leaving Padre Island."

He pushed open the doors to the two rooms. "Frank and Joe can share this room, and Ned gets one by himself."

"Thanks," Ned said.

"Come on, Frank," Joe urged. "The faster we get out of here, the faster we get to dive."

"Yeah, it's perfect weather," Buck said. "Here, let me supervise."

He followed Frank and Joe into their room and sat down on the bottom bunk bed.

Joe plopped his suitcase down on the floor. Clothes flew left and right as he rummaged through to find his bathing suit.

Buck heard a thud and looked down to see a little chamois bag land beside his feet. A set of car keys that had been fused together spilled out of the bag just then.

Buck picked up the keys and examined them. "And I thought those airport metal detectors weren't supposed to nuke your possessions."

With a tight, wan smile, Joe grabbed the keys back. Silently, he slid them back into the bag and pulled the drawstring. Frank had stopped unpacking and was eyeing him warily.

Buck looked from Frank to Joe. "Did I say something wrong—again?"

'"No," Joe said softly, breaking the tense silence. "These were my girlfriend Iola's keys for my car. She—she was killed by terrorists when my car was bombed." A sigh caught awkwardly in his throat. "This is all that was left of that day for me to remember her by."

Buck's shocked expression looked incongruous on his open, easygoing face. "Sorry, Joe. I'll—I'll put them in a safe place for you, okay?"

"Nah, you don't need to."

"Well, there've been some break-ins around here lately—you can never be too careful."

"Okay," Joe said, not really worried about anyone stealing the keys. But he did appreciate the gesture. After handing Buck the bag, he quickly changed into his swim trunks.

The four of them trooped single-file downstairs. Frank and Ned peeled off and waited by the front door as Buck took Joe into a sunny corner bedroom with two walls of sliding glass doors. He pulled open a closet and yanked aside some clothes to reveal a hidden chest of drawers. Opening the top drawer, he dropped the chamois bag inside.

"All right," Buck said, slamming the drawer shut. "Valuables tucked away, not a care in the world. Now, let's hit the beach."

With that, he and Joe stormed the front door.

"You guys ready yet?" came Mercedes's voice from the top of the stairs.

"Yep!" Nancy yelled up. She and George pushed their suitcases against a wall and spread out their sleeping bags nearby. Bess, George, and

Nancy were camping out on the living room floor. Mercedes and Kristin had the bedroom upstairs. They made their way to the front door.

"I can't believe five of us are staying here," George muttered.

Just then Mercedes came bounding down the stairs, followed by Kristin. "Sorry about the sleeping arrangements," she said.

"You're sure your parents don't mind all of us staying in their condo?" Nancy asked.

"No—as long as it's cleaned up when they come down for the summer. Besides, they know it's like this all over South Padre during vacation. People get used to it."

The four girls ran out to the jeep, where Claire and Bess were waiting for a lift to the mall. They didn't even look up as the others piled in. "The color is to die for," Claire was saying. "Of course, the only accessory I have that goes with that dress is this gorgeous diamond bracelet my mom gave me—which I keep *very* safely hidden—"

Claire kept up a steady stream of chatter until Mercedes dropped the two girls off. By the time she headed away from the mall, the skies were beginning to turn gray. Nancy looked out the window. "Do you think we'll be able to dive?"

"With Buck?" Mercedes grinned. "We'll be

going out if the Gulf freezes over and we have to rent an ice cutter."

When they got to the pier, Nancy had to let out a laugh. Buck, Frank, Joe, and Ned were clumsily pacing the dock in their flippers, looking at imaginary watches. "They know they have an audience," Nancy said.

Mercedes nodded. "Buck has a good instinct for that."

"He seems fun. You must have great times together."

"Yeah, we do, I guess." Mercedes sighed. "It's just that I can never tell if he really likes me. I mean, he flirts with me and all, but that's the way he treats everybody."

"Not *everybody*," piped up Kristin from the backseat. "Just you and—well, a few other girls. I think he does like you, sort of."

"Thanks for the encouragement," Mercedes said dryly. She pulled into a parking space.

"There they are—finally!" Buck called out in mock frustration. "Come on, it's past high tide!"

The girls raced into the rental shop, Roy's Aquatic World. Behind the counter, a ruddy-skinned man in his twenties turned around with a start. "Hi, Roy!" Mercedes called out.

Roy's face dimpled when he smiled. "Hey,

hey!" he said with a chuckle. "Your guys thought you were standing them up!"

Quickly the four girls gave their sizes and disappeared into the dressing rooms. Nancy slipped on her black wet suit, which hugged her perfectly. She scampered outside with her flippers and shoulder bag in hand.

Before long, all eight of them—Buck, Frank, Joe, Ned, Nancy, George, Mercedes, and Kristin —were motoring out into Laguna Madre in a rented boat.

"What a life!" Buck exclaimed, downing a can of cola as he flipped the rudder to the right.

Nancy couldn't agree more. She nestled her head on Ned's shoulder, feeling the warm breeze whip her hair back. The land receded slowly behind them.

"Okay. Here's a quiet spot," Buck said, throwing out an anchor. "Let's buddy up. One easterner per Texan." He looked around. "Nancy, why don't you come with me?"

Nancy felt rather than saw Mercedes stiffen slightly. She didn't feel comfortable about buddying up with Buck either, but Ned seemed to accept it with good humor.

Just then all their heads turned in unison toward the sound of a distant thunderclap.

"That's far off and won't get here," Buck said,

slipping his mask over his head. "Better hurry up or you might get wet, though." Holding his regulator in his hand, he backflipped in.

"Let's go," Mercedes said. "But remember to stick together."

Nancy went first in order to follow close behind Buck. But she immediately realized that wasn't going to be easy. Like a fish eluding a predator, Buck swam out of sight and hid behind a coral formation. Nancy had almost caught up to him when he shot out from the other end of the formation, pulling her farther and farther from the other divers.

This isn't funny, Buck, Nancy thought. She gave a quick glance backward, but the water had become dark from the approaching storm, and she could see no one.

Buck swam beside a massive coral wall that twisted and turned for about fifty feet. At the end of it, he veered out of sight once again.

Nancy was right behind him this time. And when she made the turn after Buck, she was up against the mangled, seaweed-festooned wreck of an old sailing vessel.

She swam closer, looking for Buck. In the narrow, random shafts of light that penetrated the murky water, the ship looked like the remains of an enormous wooden sea monster.

With a human victim trapped in its belly—Buck! His head had suddenly popped out from a porthole, bubbles streaming from his ripped air hose. He must have caught the hose on a jagged piece of metal.

With a couple of strong kicks, Nancy propelled herself toward him. Writhing as if in pain, he tried to squeeze his body through the narrow hole.

Stay put, Nancy wanted to shout to him. But by the time she reached him, he had managed to pull himself through. Behind his mask, she could see panic on his face.

Nancy grabbed the spare mouthpiece attached to her wet suit. She slapped it to his mouth and slowly pulled him to the surface.

The water was turbulent when they finally emerged. And Nancy was angry. "That was a pretty dangerous stunt, Buck!" she said, shouting louder than she'd intended.

"No . . . ed . . . oddy . . ." he yelled back.

At least that's what it sounded like through the sharp wind and pelting rain. "What?" Nancy asked. She put her ear closer to his mouth.

"Dead body!" Buck replied, his voice straining. *"I saw a dead body down there!"*

Chapter

Two

BUCK'S EYES FLICKERED once or twice and then closed. He's hyperventilated, Nancy realized.

Buck couldn't have picked a worse time. The rain was so heavy now that Nancy couldn't see their boat. Whitecaps were swelling and breaking all around as she hooked her arm across Buck's chest. Taking an educated guess as to where the boat was, Nancy swam carefully with Buck, gasping for mouthfuls of air over the choppy sea.

"Nancy-y-y-y!"

Nancy's eyes shot directly ahead. Ned's voice. Pulling her head way above the water, she tried to scream back, but all that came out was a strangled-sounding gasp. If only she could swim faster against the headwind, if only Buck's inert body weren't working against her . . .

Out of nowhere, a huge wave broke right over their heads. Nancy's arm instinctively tightened around Buck.

But it was too late. As she rose high into the air Buck was torn away from her.

She opened her mouth to scream—and took in at least a pint of seawater. Choking helplessly, she began to see red and white dots.

Stay conscious, Drew, she told herself. But her arms were moving with less assurance; her legs felt like lead weights.

Suddenly she felt something clamp onto her arm. Shark was the first word that flashed in her brain. Her eyes jolted open, and she let out a scream.

"Calm down, it's me!" came Buck's voice. "Where are we?"

Nancy felt a shiver of relief. "The boat's straight ahead!"

"Nancy-y-y-y!"

They followed the sound of Ned's cry. Within moments, the boat came into view.

"Ned!" Nancy managed to blurt out.

He was in the water, clinging to the side of the boat. A smile lit up his face when he saw Nancy. "Are you all right?"

Nancy hugged him with one arm and grabbed the boat with the other. "We'll talk," she said, gasping for breath.

Nancy looked up to see Mercedes, Joe, and George reaching arms down to them. Kristin was sitting with Frank on the opposite side of the boat for balance.

Joe helped Nancy hoist herself on board and then helped Ned up. The small boat heaved up on the crests of the stormy sea and fell back into the troughs. Debris from a fallen metal chest slid back and forth along the bottom—tools, maps, a crowbar.

Looking over at Buck, Nancy saw him shaking as he sat next to Mercedes, whose arm was wrapped comfortingly around his shoulder. Buck peered over at Nancy.

She met his eyes but didn't know what to say. She was relieved that he was all right, but she couldn't help but feel annoyed at him for playing dangerous games underwater and for leading them all down there in a storm.

Buck shuddered and the rain danced off his wet suit. His face was streaked with water and pale against the navy sky. "What a creep show," he said. "I—I didn't expect to see that—*thing* down there."

"It's all right, Buck," Mercedes said, helping

him remove his tank. "Calm down. I-I've never seen you like this."

"I saw a *body*, Mercedes. Some poor stiff is sucking up a faceful of sand down there in this old shipwreck, and—"

Mercedes's eyes darted suspiciously between Buck and Nancy. "Buck, this is no time for games. We have to get this boat back—"

"It's not a game—"

"I know, I know," Joe said. "You told it you were looking for a secret treasure, and it answered, 'Over my dead body!' Right?"

He laughed and started the boat, taking control of the steering wheel. The rain felt like needles driving straight into them as they bounced through the waves.

"Come on! Doesn't anybody believe me?" Buck asked incredulously.

"I don't know how you could have seen anything down there," Kristin said. "I could see barely ten feet in front of my face."

"You sure you weren't seeing someone's trash pile—old clothes that *looked* like a human shape?" Mercedes said.

Buck sighed. "Okay, maybe it *wasn't* a body. But there definitely is a wreck down there. Nancy saw that, too."

Nancy nodded. "It looked like an old pirate ship, guys. It was incredible."

Ned put his arm around Nancy. *"How* far down do you have to go before the pressure starts affecting your mind?"

As the boat approached the shore jokes were flying left and right, until Buck himself had to laugh.

But Nancy wasn't sure she should take Buck's observation lightly. And something in the set of Frank's and Joe's faces told her that they weren't going to, either.

At the pier the docked boats rose and fell jerkily with the motion of the sea. Rain pockmarked the water around the boat as Buck and Frank tied it up securely. Then they ran and joined the others in Roy's.

But Roy wasn't there now. Instead, a balding, pudgy young assistant greeted them with a baffled look. "Mr. Manvell let you out in this weather?" he said indignantly. "Highly unusual!"

"Come on, Henry," Buck said earnestly, "this is the best weather for diving. It's so dark the sharks can't see you. Besides, it gets you out of the rain."

And with that Buck turned and sauntered to

the dressing room, ignoring Henry's pinched, disapproving glare.

Nancy quickly changed out of her wet suit, trying to sort out the thoughts that bounced around in her head. Was that an ancient wreck? A body? Why was Buck so eager to go scuba diving away from everyone else? She made up her mind to go back out to the wreck as soon as she could.

Buck popped out of the men's dressing room just then. "Okay, everybody back to my place!" he shouted. He tossed his wet suit on Henry's counter. A spray of water shot up and sprinkled the clerk's glasses.

"Really!" Henry sputtered.

"Oops. Sorry, pal. By the way, you're invited, too."

Before Henry could answer, Buck raced out the door toward the white Oldsmobile convertible, where Frank and Joe were already waiting. He leaned in the front window across Joe and released a switch. Slowly the convertible top began to come down. He acted as if he loved the rain and whooped with joy. In one quick hop, he was over the side and in the backseat.

Nancy stayed inside. Ned was still in the dressing room.

"Come on, Drew!" Buck called out. "You can

ride with us. Let Ned go with the other slow pokes."

Nancy looked back in, then out again. "I don't know, they're—"

"He won't mind. Come on, hop in!"

Why not? Nancy thought, and she raced through the drizzle to the open car.

"Jump!" Buck yelled.

Nancy grabbed the side of the car. As she boosted herself over the side Buck reached up and grabbed her under her arms. Nancy giggled as she felt herself being lifted high into the air.

When she came down beside Buck, his face was dimpled with a broad grin. But when Nancy looked back toward the shop, she saw someone else who definitely wasn't amused.

Mercedes.

For a long second, Mercedes's glare held Nancy's. Suddenly Nancy wished Buck hadn't "helped" her into the car. She wished he hadn't gone scuba diving with her, either.

And she most definitely wished that she wasn't sitting next to him right then, speeding away from the girl who cared for him the most.

On the way home Frank could feel water oozing up from beneath him every time he shifted in his seat. But by the time they got to Buck's condo, the drizzle had become only a mist. With water dripping from the tips of their noses, the four of them jumped out of the White Bird, as they had christened her.

"I don't know about this," Frank said to Buck. "We soaked this car. The rental guy is going to kill us!"

Buck slammed the car door and walked to the front door of the condo. "Hey, no sweat," he replied. "The floor's so full of holes it'll all just—"

Buck stopped in his tracks. "What the—" He stared at the door, which was slightly ajar. "I didn't leave this open—"

But his words were cut off as he flung the door open and ran inside. Frank, Joe, and Nancy were hot on his heels. "Who's in here?" he shouted. "Come on, you rotten—"

Frank's attention was caught by a movement inside Buck's bedroom. Two dark figures were slipping outside through a sliding glass door.

"In there!" Frank shouted.

"Oh, no, you don't!" Buck called out, and he ran into his room.

Frank tore outside to head the intruders off. Joe and Nancy followed just in time to see the two disappear around a white-shingled house.

They were both dressed in black—one tall and broad-shouldered, the other short and thin. Buck came into view and took off after them.

Trampling over the manicured front lawn, Frank led the other two into the backyard, where they tore off after Buck.

"Where'd they go?" Frank asked urgently.

"Toward the dock," Buck called back over his shoulder as he scaled a fence.

Frank was up and over, almost on his heels. Nancy and Joe went through a gate.

They all raced through a row of backyards and out onto a dead-end street. There they stopped, not knowing which way to go.

Suddenly the sound of a powerful boat engine cut the air and made them spin to their left to a small public park that overlooked a channel.

Like a shot, a thin white cigarette boat sliced through the water. The two people inside didn't glance back, but they were both dressed in black.

Joe punched one fist into the opposite palm. "We almost had them!"

"Who do they think they are?" Buck asked, shaking his head in disbelief. "Robbing houses in the middle of the afternoon!"

"They must have known you were going out," Frank said.

"Is there anything of special value they might have been after?" Nancy asked.

Buck's eyes narrowed. "My gold watch!" He turned and ran back, not through the yards this time.

When they got to the condo, the others were waiting. "You know, you left the front door open—" Mercedes began.

But Buck pushed past her and into the house.

"Burglars," Frank said, stopping by the door. "They were here when we got back."

"Did they get anything?"

A sharp "Oh, no!" from Buck's bedroom was their answer. They ran inside to see Buck, Nancy, and Joe staring into the top drawer of the hidden dresser.

It was open and empty.

"Did they get the watch?" Frank asked.

Joe looked as if he'd just been punched in the stomach. "Iola's keys," he whispered, almost inaudibly. "They stole Iola's keys!"

Chapter

Three

A‍RE YOU SURE they're gone?" Ned asked, joining them. "Open the second drawer. Maybe you put them somewhere else."

"No," Buck answered solemnly. "My watch and Joe's keys are gone."

"What would anyone want with an old bunch of keys?" Mercedes asked.

"The keys were in a chamois bag," Buck replied. "They probably thought it was something valuable and just scooped it up with everything else." He turned to Joe and shrugged. "Sorry, buddy. I wish I could say I'd get you another set."

Joe forced a smile, but inside he felt devastated. Although Iola had died a long time ago, Joe had relived the bombing in his mind a million times. Those miserable little mutated keys had kept her alive for him. Now Joe felt as if a chunk had been ripped out of his heart.

Frank and Ned both rummaged through clothing, tennis balls, and souvenirs in the other drawers. Finally Frank looked up at his brother, his resolve strong. "We'll catch them, Joe," he said. "By the time we leave Padre Island, we'll have those keys."

Joe wanted to believe him, but he knew exactly where those keys would end up as soon as the crooks looked at them. At the bottom of some trash bag headed for the Padre Island dump.

The hectic and bizarre events of the day faded that night as they entered Dos Banditos, Buck's favorite restaurant. Accompanied by a brassy mariachi band, a dark-haired singer belted out the final chorus of a rousing Mexican folk song. An enthusiastic cheer went up around the restaurant, led by Roy Manvell, who happened to be sitting with friends near the band.

Nancy liked Dos Banditos right away—table after table of college and high school kids, all laughing and eating.

She could feel her mouth water as a waitress walked by, carrying a tray piled high with entrées for a nearby table. The plates were steaming with fragrant strips of beef and chicken, surrounded by bright vegetables, rice, refried beans, and guacamole.

"Those smell amazing!" Nancy said. "What are they?"

"Fajitas. I can't believe you haven't seen them before." Mercedes smiled as if she were teasing, but there was a hint of hostility in her voice. Nancy knew she'd have to talk to her later, reassure her about Buck. "Anyway, Dos Banditos is famous for them. They make them with beef, chicken, seafood—"

She was interrupted by the cheerful voice of another waitress. "Mercedes, thanks for doing my job for me. You guys ready to order?" Her hair shone fiery red in the festive colored lights of the restaurant, and her eyes lingered briefly on Frank as she lifted her pad and pen.

"Hi, Taryn," Mercedes said. "These are my friends Nancy, Bess, George, Frank, Joe, Ned— and you know Buck and Claire. Guys, this is Taryn Quinn. Okay, everybody ready?"

"Whoa, stay away from the chili!" a voice called from behind them. Nancy looked around to see Roy and his friends passing by on their way out. He waved to Nancy's table and winked. "It'll give you third-degree burns on your tongue."

Taryn put her hands on her hips. "Then why do you order it all the time?"

Nancy snapped her menu shut. "Okay, seafood fajitas. That's what I'm going to have."

"Just what I was going to order," George said.

"Me, too," Mercedes said.

"Make that four," came Ned's voice.

"Sounds good to me," Bess added. She straightened out the straps on her new blue sundress. "As long as it's a lot and not too messy."

Mercedes laughed. "Wait a minute. *One* of us should get something different!"

"Don't worry," Buck replied dryly. "After what I saw this afternoon, I'm not going *near* seafood." He grimaced. "Who knows what those sea creatures have been feeding on?"

"That's gross, Buck!" Claire exclaimed.

Bess looked perplexed. "What's he talking about?"

"He says he found a *body* when he was diving," Claire replied.

Bess made a sour face and looked at the menu. "Maybe I'll have chicken instead."

Taryn cast a glance around the table as she saw them all check their menus again. "I can come back," she said. "You guys need some more time to decide?"

"I *still* think it was a man's body in that shipwreck," Buck insisted, ignoring the question. "Look, I'll take you all back there tomorrow to see him, okay?"

"What if he swims away?" Frank said.

Laughter erupted from the table. By this time Taryn was impatiently fingering what looked like an antique gold coin that was hanging on a chain around her neck. "Uh, I have another table. Why don't I get them first, and—"

"No!" Buck said. "I'm starving. I'll take the chimichanga special and a side order of guacamole, extra chips."

"Okay." Taryn scribbled the order.

"That's pretty," Bess said, eyeing Taryn's necklace.

"Thanks," Taryn replied, a little coldly. She looked at Joe. "And what would you like?"

Joe stared silently at the menu, but his eyes seemed to be focused far away.

"Joe?" Nancy said. "Do you know what you want?"

"Huh?" Joe looked up with a start. He gave Nancy a puzzled look, then glanced up at Taryn. "Oh! Uh, I don't know—I'm not too hungry."

"That doesn't sound like the Joe Hardy we all know and love," Frank remarked.

"I know how he feels," George said. "I once

29

had something stolen, and it put me in a bad mood for days."

"If only we could track these guys down," Joe said sullenly. He raised his eyes to Taryn. "You live around here?"

"Yes," Taryn answered. "All my life."

"You haven't seen any suspicious types hanging out, have you?" Joe asked.

Taryn laughed. "Just Buck!"

"Seriously, Taryn," Mercedes said. "We're trying to track down a couple of people who broke into Buck's place and took some of his and Joe's stuff."

"Really?" Taryn shook her head disgustedly. "This happens every spring break. All these strangers pile in, and before you know it some slimebags are going around stealing things."

"But who could they be?" Nancy asked.

"Anyone—students, locals from nearby towns. They know they can walk around and be anonymous during the busy season." Taryn shrugged and looked at Joe sympathetically. "Sorry it had to happen to you. Why don't I bring you a Dos Banditos special? A chimichanga, a burrito, a chili relleno, and a cheese enchilada, with rice and beans—all topped with guacamole and pico de gallo. I guarantee you won't be able to think about anything else!"

"Uh, thanks," Joe said. "Well, maybe I could force that down."

"Hit it up! Hit it *up!*" Nancy yelled.

"Okay! Okay!" Planting her feet awkwardly in the sand, Bess waited for the volleyball to come down. In the light from the torches on the beach, the ball looked yellow against the night sky.

With a whack, the ball hit the heel of Bess's hand and shot toward the ground.

Instantly Ned and Nancy both dived for it. Inches from the ground, Nancy's palm slapped the ball up, but her shoulder connected with Ned's abdomen.

Ned bounced away and rolled onto his side. "Yeoow!"

"Out of bounds!" came a voice from the other side of the net.

Nancy laughed, but when she looked over at Ned, her expression changed. He was clutching his side, gritting his teeth in pain.

"Ned! Are you all right?" Nancy knelt over him. "Where does it hurt?"

Ned slowly opened his eyes. "Right"— suddenly he sat up—*"here!"* He wrapped Nancy in a bear hug and tackled her to the ground. "Revenge of the humiliated boyfriend!"

Nancy screamed and collapsed to the ground.

She struggled against Ned's tight embrace—until she felt the warm pressure of his lips against hers.

For a moment the volleyball game, the people, and the mystery were the furthest things from her mind.

Until the applause began. Around them, the other volleyball players hooted and clapped their approval.

Nancy felt her face turning red. She and Ned both sat up and nodded shyly to their friends.

"More! More!" a chant began.

"Look what you did!" Nancy said under her breath to Ned. But before she could do anything, she heard another voice in the distance.

A voice calling for help—from out in the lagoon.

"What's that?" she said.

The crowd fell silent, and the owner of the voice became clear.

"Help me!"

Nancy sprang to her feet. "It's Buck!" she said.

In an instant she, Ned, and the Hardy brothers were racing into the water. "Keep talking, Buck!" Nancy called out. "We can't see you!"

"Aaaaaagh!" Buck shouted. "Leave me alone!"

"What is it, Buck?" Joe yelled.

"Men-of-war!" came Buck's voice.

"What?" Frank said.

"Men-of-war!"

Frank froze in his tracks. "Oh, no!"

"I can't understand him," Bess said.

"Men-of-war, he's saying," Frank replied. "He must be stuck in a colony of Portuguese men-of-war jellyfish."

"Those things can be deadly!" Bess shrieked. "We have to get him!"

Chapter

Four

Nancy was already running toward a life-guard station. There, next to the tall empty white chair, a rowboat lay on its side. Nancy began dragging it toward the water. "Come on!" she called out.

Ned, Frank, and Joe helped her rush the boat into the water. As they hopped inside a crowd began to gather around.

"Help—I'm—eeeeagh!"

Buck's anguished cry made Nancy's teeth clench. "We're coming!" she shouted. "Hang in there!"

With powerful strokes, Frank and Ned rowed into the lagoon. Nancy navigated carefully, following the sound of Buck's splashing. In minutes they could see the side of his head reflected in the dim moonlight.

All around him were small black shapes. On the surface, in the darkness, they looked like harmless, discarded containers. But Nancy knew that underneath each of them stretched the poisonous, eight-foot-long tentacles of a Portuguese man-of-war.

"Here!" Ned called out, handing his oar to Joe. "Use this!"

Joe reached out over the bow of the boat, sweeping away the creatures with Ned's oar. Frank guided the boat right beside Buck. With a weak lunge, Buck tried to grab onto the boat— and fell back into the water.

Nancy reached out and clutched his arm. "Got you!" She pulled him up against the boat.

Buck raised a leg feebly over the gunwale. With Joe and Nancy's help he tumbled into the boat. "I—I don't feel so good," he mumbled. He sat down next to Nancy, shivering uncontrollably.

"You're going to be all right," Nancy reassured him.

"Did they sting you?" Frank asked.

"I th-think one of them d-did," Buck replied through chattering teeth. "I feel this—this funny sensation. L-like I'm freezing cold and boiling hot at the same time."

"Let's get him to a hospital," Nancy suggested. Even in the darkness, she could see the fear in Buck's eyes. She smiled and put a comforting arm around him.

Buck shook his head. "Y-you're pretty amazing, Drew. I—I want to say thank you, but that seems like an understatement."

Nancy smiled. "Oh, come on, it wasn't just—"

"No, no, I mean it. It's not every day that somebody saves your life—twice! There's something strange going on here."

"Mind if I ask you a question, Buck?" Ned said, his voice strained with the effort of rowing.

"Shoot."

"What were you doing swimming all alone in the middle of the night?"

Buck exhaled. "Well, I didn't start out alone; Mercedes was with me. We got into sort of an argument"—his eyes flickered briefly toward Nancy—"and we decided to cool off by taking a swim. Anyway, it didn't work. She got angry at me and swam back. I felt like being alone, so I just floated on my back for a while, closed my eyes—"

"And you woke up in the middle of those slimy little monsters," Joe said.

"It was weird," Buck went on. "First I felt one of them against my hand. That freaked me out

36

because I thought it might be a shark. So I stopped floating and tried to swim away. But as soon as I put my legs down, I felt something brush against my foot."

"Your foot?" Frank said. "Are the tentacles that long?"

Buck shook his head. "I don't know, but this wasn't a tentacle." His body gave an involuntary shudder. "It—it felt like a hand. A human hand."

An uneasy silence fell over the boat, broken only by the steady slap of the oars breaking the surface of the water.

"I know you guys must think I'm crazy," Buck said with an embarrassed smile. "I mean, I guess it could have been a fish or something. But it felt too—too *solid*. And I could have sworn I felt fingers." He looked at Frank and Joe, then turned away. "I know what you're going to say. It was the body from the shipwreck, swimming after me, right? I knew I shouldn't have told you guys—"

But Nancy could tell that Frank and Joe had no intention of joking. She recognized the look of two detectives feverishly trying to put together pieces of a puzzle.

"Buck," Frank said. "Are Portuguese men-of-war common in these waters?"

Buck knitted his brow. "That's the strange thing. Usually you only see them in the early fall—and never a whole colony like this!"

Something was wrong, Nancy thought. Something was definitely wrong. A body in a shipwreck, a theft, a colony of deadly jellyfish possibly appearing with a human in the midst of it . . .

Nothing seemed to fit—yet. Nancy vowed to herself to examine the wreck first thing the next morning. And she had a feeling she wouldn't have to twist Frank's and Joe's arms to get them to join her.

Buck rested his head on Nancy's shoulder as they pulled into shore near a growing crowd of onlookers lit by torches. "I've had some embarrassing moments in my life, but this is the worst ever," Buck said under his breath.

Nancy could feel him start to shiver as he spoke. Holding him tight to warm him, she smiled and said, "Don't worry, we'll tell them you fought off a shark."

"I think you're going to get a hero's welcome from the hometown crowd, anyway," Ned added, with an uneasy look at Nancy. She knew Ned wasn't thrilled about her embracing Buck, but she gave him a reassuring look, and his expression loosened up.

A ripple of applause spread through the crowd. Mustering his strength, Buck raised Nancy's hand in the air, waving to everybody. Then, responding to even louder cheers, he planted a kiss on her cheek.

A kiss that Nancy would have hardly noticed, except for the effect it had on one person in the crowd—Mercedes.

Her jealous glare stood out among the exuberant faces. Nancy had seen the same look when she had left the scuba place with Buck in the back seat of the White Bird. She had the sinking feeling that her welcome at Mercedes's condo was quickly wearing out.

Nancy didn't mind that Bess and George wanted to sleep late the next morning. The dive would be much more manageable with just her, Ned, and the Hardys.

At least she *thought* it would be manageable. She changed her mind when she got to the dock and saw the resentment on Joe's face.

"I don't know why we're even bothering with this," Joe grumbled. Reluctantly, he lifted his air tank and let it plop down over his shoulders.

Nancy adjusted the arms on her wet suit. She knew Joe had only one thing on his mind: finding the crooks who had stolen his keys. The last thing he wanted to do was swim around looking for an imaginary body.

"This won't take long, Joe," Nancy said. "With Buck in the hospital, we know he can't pull any tricks on us."

"Look, we're going to track down the keys as soon as we check this thing out," Frank assured him. "I mean, what if Buck was right?"

"Sure." Joe snuffled sarcastically. "Let's just get it over with."

With that, he hopped into their rented boat, followed by Ned, who started the engine and took the steering wheel.

The boat sputtered a few times and then glided out across the Gulf. Nancy watched as the pier faded into the distance.

"Lucky I looked at the compass the last time we were out here," Ned remarked.

Nancy put her arm around his shoulder. "My hero," she teased.

The water became darker as they got farther out. Ned turned down the throttle and maneuvered the boat slowly around. "If I remember right, this is where we were."

"Do you remember how to get to the wreck, Nancy?" Frank asked.

"I can try." Nancy pulled on her mask and flipped in. Visibility was much better than it had been the day before, and in the distance she could see the long coral wall that she and Buck had swum beyond. Looking over her shoulder, she made sure that Ned, Frank, and Joe were behind her. She retraced her path along the wall, turning to the right just beyond it.

And there, huge in the shimmering half light of the deep sea, was the ancient wreck. It had sunk straight up and down. A barnacle-encrusted mast rose from it, cracked badly in the middle and swaying with the current. Brightly colored fish swam out of the porthole that Buck had shattered.

There must have been another way Buck had gotten inside the ship before he swam to the porthole.

She propelled herself along the length of the ship, scanning the algae-covered deck. Right away her search was rewarded.

An entire section of the hull was missing. There was more than enough room for them to swim around and view the interior of the ship with the flashlights they had brought.

As Nancy neared the hole she knew that it had to have been very dark in there when Buck went in. For him to have seen a body—or *whatever* he saw—he must have swum right up to it.

Not exactly a pleasant thought.

Nancy waited for the others to catch up, and together they entered the hole. She and Ned went off to the left, lights bobbing, Frank and Joe to the right.

It was creepy, Nancy thought. A school of tiny fish fluttered past, scared from their hiding place. Metal and wooden planks jutted out from the walls, casting eerie silhouettes.

Nancy gulped. Minutes earlier she'd been looking forward to this dive. Finding Buck's "body" was going to be exciting and intriguing.

Now she wasn't so sure.

Seaweed, sand, fish—*none* of it resembled a body, Joe thought. Buck must have been seeing things. A few feet away Frank was shining his light into all the corners of the ship's hold.

This was getting ridiculous. Joe reached down halfheartedly and scooped up a handful of sand. In the light that came in through the ship's hull, the sand billowed and floated back downward, in gleaming specks of white and pink.

And gold.

Joe's eyes widened. The gold glimmer couldn't have been sand. It was too big, too shiny.

But by now, whatever it was had disappeared into the ocean floor. Joe dug his hand back in and let a clump of sand sift through.

Nothing.

He dug out another clump, and another. Sticks, pieces of moss—but no gold.

Frustrated, Joe swept his arm in a wide arc through the sand. Out of the corner of his eye, he saw Frank swimming over.

And when he looked back down, there it was, perfectly preserved and glinting with the beam of Frank's flashlight.

The glint of a solid-gold coin.

Chapter

Five

THESE TANKS DON'T HOLD very much oxygen, do they?" Joe was frustrated as he and the others climbed back aboard their motorboat.

"Maybe you can rent gills next time," Frank said. "Now, come on, let's see that coin."

The boat's engine roared as they sped back toward the pier. While Ned manned the steering wheel, Frank, Joe, and Nancy gathered around Joe.

"There's *got* to be buried treasure there!" Joe insisted. "I mean, did you get a load of that rig? A classic pirate ship, no question!"

Frank shook his head. "I don't know, Joe. We searched every square inch."

He held up the coin. It was old, all right—so

old that its markings were too worn to distinguish where it had come from or what year it had been minted. "Maybe you're right, Joe," Nancy said. "But if there *was* a treasure there, looters probably swam off with it long ago."

"I'm not so sure," Ned piped up.

Joe smiled. "I knew somebody would have to be on my side."

"I think that body Buck saw was Long John Silver," Ned went on. "The poor guy probably got tired waiting for Buck to return and took the treasure over to Davy Jones's locker."

"Very funny," Joe replied. "I'm going to go back and look some more for this thing—and if you guys are nice to me, I *may* cut you in on some of it!"

A few feet from the pier, Ned turned off the engine and let the boat drift the rest of the way. Frank helped him tether it to the dock, and the four of them hopped off.

"I never thought I'd have to drag *you* out of the water to look for your keys," Frank said.

Joe held open the side entrance to Roy's. "I'm going after those keys, all right. But as soon as we track down *those* guys, I'm right back here. And I'm going over every inch of that wreck!"

From behind the counter, Roy grinned. "Don't tell me you guys discovered an old ship!"

Joe squared off and faced him. "You mean someone else found it?"

"Oh, I don't know if it's the same one," Roy answered. "Every few months someone comes in with a sighting. Most of the time it's an old rowboat. Once or twice it was one of *my* boats—"

"No one ever mentioned an old pirate-type vessel?" Joe asked.

Roy laughed. "Oh, sure. A few people have told me about those. Must be dozens of them out there, judging from the different descriptions. Everyone thinks there's hidden treasure in them. You can almost read the dollar signs in their eyes."

Frank could see Joe flinch defensively at that last remark. "Well . . . you never know," he said, heading for the dressing room.

"True," Roy answered. "Especially around here, with all the pirate trade that passed by in the old days. In the early seventies some guys actually did dig up buried treasure worth three million dollars."

Frank stopped in his tracks. Nancy threw him a glance, and he knew they were thinking the same thing: Maybe Joe's idea wasn't so far-fetched.

Joe was slack-jawed. "Three million—"

"'Course, they found that on land," Roy went on. He shrugged and added, "If I were you, I'd forget about those ships and go after old Jean Laffite's loot. Nobody's found that yet."

"Jean *who?*" Ned said.

"Laffite. Big honcho in the pirate world. The guy sails to Padre Island—of course, it wasn't called that back then—buries his treasure under some stone, carves the words *Dig Deeper* into it, and never lives to come back and get it! Incredible, huh? I tell you, there are some fools who've spent years trying to track that down."

"No kidding," Joe said, fascinated.

Frank could tell that Roy was in his element. With an expansive gesture, he pulled a pile of newspaper clippings and photos out from under his desk. "I can show you some great articles—"

"Thanks, Roy," Frank quickly said. "But we have to get going!" Under his breath, he urged, "Come on, Joe. We can worry about our fortune later."

"Hey, moneybags!" Roy called out as they all ran toward the dressing rooms. "Don't forget to pay me on the way out!"

The boat-rental agent gave Nancy a wary look. "Sure, I rent cigarette boats—but why should I let you look at my records?"

"Please, sir, we believe some thieves are using one as a getaway boat," Frank replied.

The man nodded and thrust an open loose-leaf book toward Nancy and Frank. "I guess it won't do any harm. All the rentals are right on this page—the numbers that begin with CG." Ned and Joe looked over their shoulders.

With a glimmer of hope, Nancy opened the book. They'd already been to three other rental places without any success. Maybe their luck was about to change.

She turned to the log for the day before. They had seen the crooks at about five o'clock, so she ran her fingers down to the afternoon rentals:

$$4:02 \quad CG=102$$
$$4:07 \quad CG=35$$
$$4:14 \quad CG=79$$
$$4:17 \quad CG=50$$
$$4:25 \quad CG=92$$
$$4:31 \quad CG=55$$
$$4:40 \quad CG=100$$
$$4:47 \quad CG=66 \ldots$$

Nancy's shoulders sagged as she read more and more. "I guess you rent a lot of cigarette boats," she remarked.

"Oh, yeah," the agent said. "They're real popular around here."

"So we've noticed," Joe said dryly.

Frank leaned over the counter. "You don't happen to remember two guys, one short and thin, one tall and well-built, each wearing a baseball hat and black clothes—"

The agent furrowed his brow, then smoothed down a few strands of red hair across his otherwise bald head. "Hard to say. I mean, so many people go through here. Can you give me a better description? Did you notice any markings on the hull?"

"No," Nancy answered. "Unfortunately, they left too quickly for us to catch any details."

"Hmm. I'm afraid you're going to have a problem, kids. There are a lot of those boats rented around here. And you don't even know it was rented. Plenty of day-trippers come to South Padre, you know."

It was the same story they'd heard at the other places. Nancy could feel the gloom thickening around Joe as he turned from the counter.

"Well, thanks for letting us look," Ned said. "And if you remember anything that might help us, just call this number, okay?"

He took a piece of paper out of his pocket,

wrote Buck's number on it, and gave it to the man.

The man shrugged. "I'll try, but don't count on anything."

The four of them left the shop and hopped into the White Bird. Joe didn't say a word.

"Where to? What do we do now?" Ned asked, driving. "Keep going along the coast?"

Joe looked off into the distance, squinting into the wind from the open road. "Nah," he said. "It doesn't make sense. We're not going to find them."

"You never know," Frank replied. "We've been in worse situations—"

"No, Frank," Joe said quietly. "That's not the point. This is supposed to be our vacation. All we've done so far is chase after a body that doesn't exist and a sentimental—souvenir. I can live without those keys. They're not going to bring Iola back, anyway."

Frank shrugged. "If you say so, Joe."

"I say so. Let's go to the beach. Maybe we can find Bess and George over by Mercedes's."

At the next traffic light, Ned turned toward the shore. Nancy felt bad for Joe. She knew he was crushed. "I think you made the right decision, Joe," she said, turning around to talk to him. "But I know it must have been tough."

Joe nodded. Nancy wasn't sure, but for a moment she thought she saw tears pooling in his eyes. With a stoic smile, he said, "Hey, life is for the living, right? Besides, we're going to leave Padre Island with Jean Laffite's fortune. Right?"

Nancy grinned. "Right, Joe."

Within minutes, Ned was pulling up to a parking lot in front of a sprawling condo complex of identical, attached stucco units. Nancy led them through the entrance gate, into a courtyard, and then onto the beach just beyond.

A wall of sound greeted them—blaring boom boxes, rowdy volleyball and touch-football games, and the crashing of waves against the shore.

"How are we going to find them?" Ned asked, bewildered.

Joe's eyes darted around the beach, glancing at the girls. "Who cares?" he answered.

Nancy grabbed his arm. "Come on. Bess told me where to meet them."

She led them onto the sand, weaving through many bodies toward a high, white lifeguard chair. Several feet away, sunning themselves on four enormous beach towels, were Mercedes, Bess, George, and Claire.

As they got closer Nancy could hear Bess's and Claire's voices.

"Blond?" Bess asked rapturously.

"Like strands of gold," Claire answered.

"Blue eyes?"

"Unbelievably blue."

"Great body?"

"I'm telling you, Bess—*hunk* wasn't a strong enough word for him."

"Sounds good to me!" Nancy interrupted. "What did you do with him?"

The four girls turned. All but Mercedes returned her smile. "It's about time!" Bess said. "Any luck?"

Frank shook his head. "Zero for two. No body, no keys."

"Just as well," George said wryly. "Now you can join our discussion about the phantom lifeguard."

"Bruce," Claire interjected.

As the boys sprawled out on the towels Nancy sat down carefully in a small space next to Bess. She tried not to notice the chilly sidelong glance Mercedes gave her. "So," she said cheerfully, "who *is* this guy, anyway?"

Claire rolled her eyes skyward. "For three of the five days I was here before you came, he sat in that chair every day, ten to six. You notice that this side of my face is twice as tan as the other? That's because I was always facing him. Anyway, we dated once, just casually, but a couple of days ago when I showed up this new guy had taken his place."

Nancy looked up to see a nondescript lifeguard climbing up to the top of the chair. "Did you find out where he went?" she asked.

Claire shrugged. "He was probably discovered by some Hollywood agent or something. Who knows? Guys *that* good-looking don't stay lifeguards very long."

Suddenly Claire gasped. "Hey! What do you think you're—"

"Come on, star eyes!" Mercedes said, pulling on Claire's arm. "We're getting wet, whether you like it or not!"

Claire's squeals of protest were drowned out by everyone else's screams of joy as they all rushed toward the surf.

For the first time, Nancy felt that she was finally on vacation.

There, that looks pretty good, Nancy thought late the next morning. She backed away from the bathroom mirror, cocking her head one way, then the other. In the light from the vanity the blond highlights in her red hair shimmered.

It definitely felt good not to be thinking about crime and intrigue.

Nancy dropped her hairbrush when she heard a piercing scream from the courtyard. She rushed to the back door and flung it open.

"Nancy!" It was Claire. She ran inside, her face white under its tan.

"What happened?" Nancy asked.

Claire grabbed Nancy's arms. "It's my diamond bracelet! I hid it in a safe place, and now—now it's gone!"

Chapter

Six

Nancy led Claire inside and sat her down on the couch. "Are you sure you didn't just misplace it?" she asked.

"N-no," Claire said, openly sobbing. "I take it wherever I go, hidden in a secret compartment of my jewelry box. It's a family heirloom, and my mother always told me to put it in a safe-deposit box, but I always thought—what a silly thing to do—leave this gorgeous piece to rot in some cold bank. Anyway, I look at it every time I put on my jewelry. I saw it yesterday, but when I checked it just now, the compartment was empty!"

"Was there anything else gone?"

Claire nodded, drying her eyes. "Some savings

bonds my father had bought for me, two necklaces—they left all the stuff that wasn't expensive."

"Sounds like an inside job," Nancy mused. "Someone who knows the layout of your room and has access to it."

"Fabulous." Claire's shoulders slumped. *"That* narrows it down to about fifty people. Half my high school class has been in and out of my condo. I've been putting up anyone who needs a place to stay for spring vacation."

Nancy sighed. This wasn't going to be easy. "Well, did any of them actually see you wear it?"

"No—I mean, I don't think so. I only wore it once, on my date with Bruce—"

"The lifeguard?"

"Yes. But he never came to my place. In fact, to tell the truth, my 'date' was really just a party where we hung out together. He never took me home. I don't even think he knows where I live. Besides, if he does, he'd never do anything like that. He's such a *nice* guy."

"Mm-hm," Nancy said noncommittally. "Well, it could be someone in the condo. Maybe you could ask some of the residents—"

"Oh, Nancy, I just can't *believe* anyone who knows me would do this." Claire stood up and began pacing. "And besides, even if you're right, I could never approach any of these people myself. Could you help me? Bess told me all about you—how you're a private investigator and all. She says you're the best. Please."

It never failed, Nancy thought. Just when things were calming down . . . She shrugged her shoulders.

"Okay," she said. "We're on. We'll head out to the beach and ask some questions."

Nancy strolled out on the sand where most of the sunworshipers were gathered around a little man whose bald head was bright pink.

"Welcome to the Ultimate Frisbee semifinals! Will the Howard Hondos and the Fulton Freethrowers take the field?" he asked.

A cheer went up from the crowd as the small man's voice boomed out over the loudspeakers.

"So you weren't in the house at all yesterday?" Nancy asked a tall, willowy, blond girl named Crystal, whom she knew was staying at Claire's.

"No, I was on the beach all day and dancing all night," she answered. "Why?"

"Someone broke into Claire's room. I thought you might know if a stranger was there at any time."

"Oh, how terrible! I have no idea—"

"You don't know anything about a guy named Bruce? A lifeguard?"

Crystal scrunched her eyebrows. "I know who you mean. Does Claire know him?"

"A little bit. Did you ever see him around the condo?"

"Nope." She laughed. "Even if he'd been there once, I'd be surprised if he could find his way again."

Nancy looked at her quizzically.

Crystal said with an impish look, "He isn't exactly a brain surgeon, if you know what I mean."

Nancy smiled. "Thanks, Crystal."

"Score," blared the announcer's voice.

Nancy turned to watch the competition, where the Fulton team was jumping up and down in triumph. Just then she felt a warm breath on her ear as she heard a gruff voice whisper, "I'll lay ya five-to-one odds on the Howard team."

She spun around and was nose to nose with Frank. "Don't tell me I scared you," he said.

"Of course not," Nancy said calmly, taking a step back and hoping the goosebumps on her arms weren't showing. "So, where have you and the guys been?"

"Ned took some of Buck's stuff over to the

hospital, Joe decided to check out a couple more cigarette boats, and I've been getting some background on Buck," Frank replied.

"Buck? Why?"

"I've got some questions about the attack by the colony of Portuguese men-of-war. What if, I thought, someone put those jellyfish out there— someone who has it in for Buck?"

Nancy scratched her head. "It seems a little fishy." Frank groaned at the bad joke. "But Buck is so harmless. What could he have done?"

"Nothing, according to everyone I've spoken to. But his *father* has made a few enemies around here. There's a reason Buck can afford a beachfront condo of his own. Seems that his dad, Cord Buchanan, was involved in some pretty shady real-estate deals." He shrugged. "Maybe some of that bad feeling has trickled down to his son."

Frank was tapped on the shoulder, and he turned to face a gangly, solemn teenage guy with dark, close-cropped hair. The stranger adjusted his wire-rimmed glasses and said, "You were the guy asking questions about the Buchanan family, right?"

"Yes." Frank stuck out his hand and said, "Frank Hardy. And this is Nancy Drew."

The stranger's eyes darted from side to side as

he quickly shook Frank's hand. "Cranston. Rupert Cranston. Let's move somewhere private."

Rupert led them to a secluded spot behind a bathhouse. Looking over his shoulder, he said, "Are you reporters?"

"No," Frank answered.

"Good. They always distort everything." He lowered his voice. "Anyway, I have all the dirt on the Buchanans you'll ever need. You see, my family is *the* Padre Island Cranstons."

Frank and Nancy stared at him blankly.

Rupert looked annoyed. "Cranston? Of Cranston Oil and Gas, the oldest fuel company in southeastern Texas? Oh, never mind, you must be from out of state. Anyway, everyone in Texas knows about the feud between the Cranstons and the Buchanans. It's been going on since Buck's granddaddy tried to drive my granddaddy out of business years ago. And Buck's dad was even worse. You can ask anyone who lives here—" With a sweep of his hand, he indicated the shops that lined the beach. "He swindled Mr. Quinones, who owns Abe's Bait and Tackle. . . ."

"So, you're not crazy about Buck," Nancy said.

Rupert's features softened. "Oh, Buck's all right, actually. We were in school together, from kindergarten right through Phelps College. When we were little, he was the only kid who didn't think I was weird." He let out a strange, high-pitched giggle. "I collect unusual animals. Buck was kind of into helping me; he used to bring me lizards and stuff."

"Uh-huh," Frank said. "Well, thanks for the info, Rupert. You've been a great help."

"No problem. If you ever need anything else, give me a call." He handed them a card with his phone number on it, underneath the words "Rupert Cranston—Inventor, Computer Consultant —Have Ideas, Will Travel." "See you," he said.

As he walked away, Frank raised an eyebrow. "What a character."

"You think *he's* involved in this?" Nancy asked.

"Doesn't seem likely. But maybe we should check out this Quinones guy."

Nancy and Frank trotted out to the white-shingled Abe's Bait and Tackle Shop, which stood at the end of a row of stores. Beyond it, a causeway stretched from South Padre Island to the mainland.

"Is Abe here?" Frank asked as he walked through the screen door.

A rail-thin, completely bald man put down a fishing reel and looked up. He smiled with his mouth, but it didn't reach his eyes, which looked bored and impatient. "I'm Abe. What can I do for you?"

"We're, uh, students at Phelps College," Frank replied, "and we're working on a newspaper feature about the Buchanan family. We were wondering—"

"Ho-o-old it right there," Quinones cut in. He snorted once. "I think you're coming to the wrong place. There ain't nothin' I can tell you about ol' Cord Buchanan you can print in a newspaper—at least a *decent* sort of paper, if you know what I mean."

Nancy acted startled. "Oh? Did you know Mr. Buchanan personally?"

Quinones's eyes were steely and focused far away. "I'll say I did. I used to own some of this here land." He pointed out the window to the beach. "It was the Quinones family legacy— heck, my family has lived here since back when Texas was a place you only went to if your covered wagon got lost. They waded across the Rio Grande from Mexico and watered the land of Texas with the sweat of their brows."

"You *owned* this?" Frank asked. "What happened?"

"Well," Quinones continued, "it wasn't so impressive looking a while back—just a scrubby ol' sandbar. But it was mine. While them others were building, building, I just let people swim and fish here, no problem. 'Course, me and my wife had the kids, then she died, and I had this—well, sort of a drinking problem. Before I knew it, I was plumb broke. Anyhow, this Buchanan fella, all scrubbed and wearing a fancy suit, comes over and tells me he wants to buy my land—for enough money to feed and clothe my family for a year. Agreed to let me keep running the shop rent-free for five years. Sounded like a good deal to me. Personally, I thought the guy was crazy, gypping himself! So I said yes."

"And then South Padre Island became a real hot spot," Nancy said.

"The land values shot through the roof. I tell ya, the money Buchanan paid me was peanuts compared to what he got subdividing the land. I could have become a millionaire, just sitting here in the shop, doing nothing." Quinones shook his head sadly. "Who'd have thought . . ."

"Obviously Buchanan did," Frank said.

Quinones sighed. "Well, at my age, I can't get too worked up about it. We was never rich, but my daughter's doin' okay, and business ain't bad." A craggy smile spread across his face as he looked from Frank to Nancy. "I guess you kids must be good reporters. You got your information out of me, didn't you?"

"Thanks, Mr. Quinones," Nancy said with a smile. She and Frank turned to leave.

"And don't mention my name in the article," Quinones called after them.

"Don't worry, we won't," Frank said over his shoulder.

As they walked back across the highway to the beach Frank asked, "What do you think?"

"Well, he has an ax to grind, but I have a feeling Quinones and Cranston are not the only ones," Nancy answered.

"Yeah, Buck's dad sure wasn't out to win any popularity contests, huh?" Frank and Nancy stood at the head of the beach, looking out over the water.

A familiar voice cut through their thoughts. "Hey, you guys. Don't just stand there."

It was Bess, and next to her, George. They pointed down the beach to a small crowd that was moving toward the water. In the center of the crowd were Ned and Joe, carrying what looked like a motor scooter on skis.

"What is that?" Nancy said.

"Buck's jet ski, I guess," Frank said. "Joe was going to ask him if he could use it. Guess he succeeded."

"Does he know how?"

"We'll see. . . ."

The four of them ran down to the surf.

A noise like that of a lawn mower sliced the air. Nancy and Frank watched as Joe swam out with the ski and shakily climbed on top.

"Go for it!" Ned called out.

Joe did. He jerked forward as the ski took off but righted himself almost instantly. He bent his knees and leaned forward, shooting across the water at top speed.

Nancy caught on first, and her eyes popped wide in horror. Joe couldn't stop. He was heading south at breakneck speed—on a collision course with an ominous black jetty!

Chapter

Seven

FRANK RACED TOWARD the water. "Jump, Joe!"

But he knew as he was shouting that his words were of no use. The noise of the jet ski was drowning out his voice.

Frank's face was pale with fright and disbelief. Joe, hundreds of yards away, was clinging onto the handgrip as if frozen. He was steering right for the jetty.

The sound of the collision when it came was all the more sickening because of its anticipation. Frank watched in horror as shards of metal and fiberglass sprayed into the air. They seemed to fall in slow motion as Frank stood rooted to his spot, watching.

A sudden hush fell over the crowd. Everyone turned to look out to sea, stunned.

Frank found his legs finally and chased along the beach, followed by the others. It must have been two hundred yards to the jetty, but they covered it in seconds. They looked out at the pieces of the jet ski, floating on the water's surface, jagged and lifeless.

Frank forced his eyes to the left edge of the debris—and cringed. There was no mistaking Joe's gleaming blond hair.

And there was no mistaking Joe's voice. "Don't just stand there. Come on in, the water's beautiful!"

"Joe!" Frank bellowed. Relief flashed across his face, and he plunged in the water to join his brother.

In minutes the two of them were back on the sand. Strangers who had been watching drifted back to their activities.

Nancy grabbed Joe's hand. Bess and George joined them. "What happened?" they all asked at once.

"I don't know," Joe said, shaking his head. "I couldn't control it, no matter what I tried. I didn't want to ruin Buck's ski, but there was nothing I could do, so I jumped off."

"Well, now that you're safe and sound, there's only one problem left," Frank said.

"What's that?" Joe asked.

"Who's going to break the news to Buck about his ski?"

After a short trip to their condos for a change of clothes, the six of them paid Buck an early-afternoon visit.

As they entered his hospital room they saw Mercedes seated on a chair next to the bed. With a smile, Buck sat up, but immediately his smile turned to a grimace. "Ugh, my head. It feels like a sumo wrestler just sat on it."

"You poor thing," Mercedes said, gently stroking his forehead.

"Can I get you anything?" Bess asked.

"Sure, Bess," Buck replied. But as he sank back into his pile of pillows his eyes were on Nancy. "Would you mind getting me some water? I think I'm dehydrated."

Nancy poured him a glass of water from his ice-filled pitcher. As she handed him the glass Buck smiled gratefully and pointed toward the foot of the bed. "I think you might have to crank me up, too."

"Yes, sir," Nancy said. Bess did that task, cranking him up until the mattress was in an upright position. Mercedes carefully put an arm around Buck's shoulders and eased him up.

"Mmm, all the comforts of home," Buck said, and he sighed dramatically.

Out of the corner of her eye, Nancy noticed Mercedes pull away and fold her arms.

"So," Nancy said, "I think Joe has something to say."

Joe looked uncomfortable as he launched into the story of the jet ski. "We'll pay you back," he finished up.

"No problem," Buck said. "Are you sure *you're* all right? You don't look too terrific."

"I feel lousy about wrecking it," Joe said.

"The only thing bothering him is how much the thing is going to cost," Frank teased.

"Forget it," Buck said, a bit too forcefully.

"Well, that's really nice of you, Buck," Joe said.

"Generous to a fault," Mercedes added, with a slight edge to her voice.

Just then there was a knock at the door. A nurse popped her head in and said, "Visiting hours are over."

"Aw, you're not kicking them out, are you, Nurse Davenport?" Buck asked sweetly. "They're treating me better than you do!"

With a bemused look, the nurse said, "Now, don't be selfish, Mr. Buchanan. You *are* being released tomorrow morning, don't forget." She backed out and shut the door behind her.

"That's what she thinks," Buck said under his breath. "The doctor's coming in a few hours. He just *happens* to be a friend of my dad's. He says if I can walk a straight line, I'm out of here—now."

"That'll be a good excuse for some kind of blowout," Joe said.

"I hope I'm up to it," Buck said, clutching his forehead in mock agony. "I'm not the man I used to be."

"Why don't I believe that?" George said with a grin as she and the others stood up to go.

The four girls all gave Buck a kiss before they left, and he pretended to swoon into a blissful sleep.

Outside in the parking lot, Nancy walked with Ned to the White Bird, followed by Frank and Joe. Bess and George headed for Mercedes's jeep.

"Uh, hang on a second," Mercedes said pointedly. "Listen, you guys wouldn't mind if Nancy and I drove back alone, would you?" She smiled at Bess and George. "We need to have a little— girl talk."

"Oh," Bess said, trying to look as if she understood. "Sure, no problem."

Nancy gave Ned a quick kiss goodbye. She climbed into the Jeep with Mercedes, and Bess and George piled into the White Bird.

Nancy buckled herself in and watched the old white car pull away. Silently, Mercedes inserted the key into the ignition, but she didn't turn it. Instead she leaned back into her seat, exhaled, and looked at Nancy. "You know, I'm the kind of person who likes to have everything out in the open."

"Great," Nancy replied with a smile. "Me, too."

Mercedes nodded. "All right. Then tell me one thing—are you after Buck?"

Before Nancy could say anything, a rush of words came flooding out of Mercedes's mouth. "Because if you are, Nancy Drew, I sure would appreciate if you didn't humiliate me by staying in my house. I mean, I—I can understand how you'd be attracted to him, really I can, but you have to understand how I feel—"

"Oh, Mercedes," Nancy said, meeting her friend's wounded gaze. "I'm not after Buck, I promise! I mean, he's good-looking and all, but *Ned* is my boyfriend, and nothing's going to change that. Buck and you both know that."

"It's Buck's fault, then, isn't it?" Mercedes was

seething with anger now. "He acts like Ned doesn't exist, right in front of both of us!"

"I don't think he means anything by it, Mercedes. That's why Ned doesn't mind. I think Buck just gets a little . . . overaffectionate and needs lots of attention and reassurance."

Mercedes nodded and looked away. "I—I guess sometimes I just wish he were a little overaffectionate with *me.*" A faint smile flickered on her face. "Thanks, Nancy."

"For what?"

"For not yelling at me when I accused you."

Nancy smiled. "Don't worry. I understand."

She and Mercedes exchanged a warm glance. Mercedes started up the Jeep and pulled onto the highway. "I don't know why I get so worked up over this guy," she said. "I mean, he obviously doesn't appreciate it."

"Well, if it doesn't work out between you two, there are"—Nancy looked out the window at the beach, where a group of guys were playing football—"plenty of hunks on the sand."

Mercedes rolled her eyes. "The trouble is, the hunks are too busy being in love with themselves. It's hard to find a cute guy who's smart and nice. You should see the nerds I end up with some-times." Suddenly her eyes fixed on a nearby ice-cream stand. "Uh-oh, I feel an emergency pit-stop coming on. What flavor do you like?"

"How about strawberry swirl?" Nancy answered, reading from the list of flavors on a wooden board at the side of the stand.

The Jeep screeched to a halt. "Be right back!"

Mercedes hopped out of the car and ran to the ice-cream stand. Nancy sat back and watched as three guys sat down at a picnic table, their cones piled too high with ice cream.

"Hey, hey!" she heard a voice call out. "Yo, Cranston! There's your girlfriend! What's her name?"

One of the other two laughed. The third one blushed. Nancy recognized him instantly as Rupert.

"Her name is Mercedes, Mark," Rupert corrected his friend.

"Is it true you went out with her?" Mark asked.

Rupert looked shocked. "No. Who told you that?"

Mark raised his eyebrows mischievously. "Rumor has it you invited her up to see your Portuguese man-of-war collection one evening."

A sudden shiver shot through Nancy.

"Very funny," Rupert replied. He sighed and looked toward the ice-cream stand. "I wish she would go out with me, but all she can think about is Buchanan." He practically spat out the last word. "Besides, I don't have that collection anymore, so you can stop giving me grief about it."

"Oh, no!" Mark said, feigning dismay. "Don't tell me! Your South American tarantulas got loose and ate them?"

Rupert's face became very serious. "Look, I really don't want to talk about it, okay?"

Mark held up his hands defensively. "Okay, sorry I asked."

But Nancy wasn't sorry at all. Her mind was racing. Rupert had had a collection of deadly jellyfish. Rupert had reason to hate Buck. Now Rupert's jellyfish were gone.

Maybe Buck's encounter the other night wasn't an accident after all!

And what about the other "accident"? Did the controls on Buck's new jet ski just *happen* to be jammed? Did Joe walk into a setup that wasn't meant for him?

It didn't seem right. Nancy couldn't imagine why anyone would want to kill Buck. And Rupert didn't seem like the killer type.

But you never knew. . . .

Late that afternoon the surf had kicked up to perfect bodysurfing conditions. Nancy was determined to take advantage. She and George tackled the waves as Bess and Claire sat on the sand and watched. Bess didn't want to get her suit wet, and Claire was still too upset to want to join in.

"Here it comes!" George shouted, pointing out over the water. "The perfect wave!"

Sure, Nancy thought. Perfect *tidal* wave. She thrust herself forward as it swept over her and felt her arms being pulled one way and her legs the other. For a second, it seemed as though her body would split in two. Then, with an abrupt, involuntary kick, her legs sailed over her head. It was useless fighting it. She held her breath and tumbled.

"Way to go, Nancy!"

Bess's voice was the first thing Nancy heard when she washed up on shore. As the remains of the huge wave retreated she staggered to her feet and looked at George. "How come *you* don't ever get caught underneath?"

George tried to act bored. "Talent, I guess."

They both turned when they heard Mercedes shout, "Come on, it's four. I just called Buck. He got sprung from the hospital."

"I thought you were going to pick him up," George said.

Mercedes shrugged. "Ned was with me when I

called him and said he'd go get him. I gave him the keys to the Jeep."

Bess and Claire were already packed, so the five girls walked back up to Mercedes's condo.

Bess pulled the door open, and instantly her face lit up. "Hey! Look what came while you were out."

In every corner of the living room was a bright, overflowing bouquet of flowers. The biggest one was by the door. On it, a card hung from a long passion flower.

"How sweet! Buck must have sent these," Mercedes said, reaching eagerly for the card.

"That's one nice thing about having so many people in your house," George remarked. "Kristin must have been here to accept the delivery."

Mercedes ripped open the envelope and read the card. Her smile vanished.

"What's it say?" Bess asked.

Mercedes let Bess take the card from her hand, and listlessly she walked into the kitchen.

Nancy read over Bess's shoulder: *To Nancy, From Buck.*

"Uh-oh," Bess muttered.

Nancy sighed. "My feelings exactly. I'd better talk to her."

But before Nancy could move, a scream from

another condo made her freeze. She turned and ran. By the time she got to the right apartment, Mercedes, Claire, Bess, and George were right behind her.

A freckled blond girl stood at the outside door, looking in. Her eyes were wide with terror.

Inside, the floor was strewn with sheets, shredded pillows, and clothes. A bureau stood against one wall like a miniature gutted building, its drawers pulled out and overturned nearby.

"Jennifer, are you okay?" Mercedes asked, putting an arm around the girl's shoulders.

Jennifer nodded blankly.

"Did you have anything valuable?" Nancy asked.

Without saying a word, Jennifer pointed to the far wall. A pure white rectangle showed against the off-white wall, where a painting must have once hung.

In the center of the rectangle was a wall safe with its door hanging open!

Chapter

Eight

WHAT DID YOU have in there?" Nancy asked.

"What *didn't* I have? Two gold necklaces, a sapphire ring with matching earrings, bracelets, a string of pearls . . ." Jennifer walked into the room and plopped down on a sofa. "I can't go on. It's making me too depressed."

Just then there was a clatter of footsteps in the hallway. "What's going on?"

Nancy popped her head out to see Frank and Joe racing toward them. She stepped aside to let the brothers look into the room.

For a moment they just stared silently.

"When could this have happened, Jennifer?" Nancy asked.

Jennifer shrugged. "This morning, this afternoon—I don't know. I was at the beach all day watching the Ultimate Frisbee contest."

"Is anyone else staying here?" Frank pressed.

"Sure, a whole bunch of my friends," Jennifer replied. "But they were all with me on the beach."

"And no one else knows about the safe?" Nancy continued.

"No. I should say, nobody *suspicious*—just Mercedes and my boyfriend—"

"*And* Bruce," Mercedes added.

"Bruce?" Jennifer didn't have the slightest hint of recognition in her eyes.

Nancy turned to Mercedes. "You mean the lifeguard?"

"Bruce?" Bess said in disbelief, casting a quick glance at Claire, whose mouth hung open.

"Yes," Mercedes answered. "Don't you remember, Jennifer? A couple of weeks ago Bruce came over to us at the beach and told us he was worried about his watch and his ring."

Jennifer's face sank. "Oh, no. I remember now. I told him I could hide them for him in my wall safe. How stupid of me!"

"Did he know where you lived?" Nancy asked.

"No. Besides, he would never have done anything. I mean, he was such a pussycat."

"Oh, Bruce," Bess and Claire said in unison.

"Another dream shattered," George commented.

Nancy sighed and looked over the ransacked room. Now she had another robbery to investigate besides Claire's. "Jennifer, the best thing you can do is notify the police right now."

"Okay," Jennifer said glumly, and she went to dial.

Soon a loud horn blared from the front of the condo. Mercedes rushed over to Jennifer's window. "Hi, Buck! We'll be right there as soon as we change," she called out, then she turned back into the apartment. "How about coming to dinner with us, Jennifer? That'll make you feel better."

"No, thanks," Jennifer replied. "I have to wait for the police. Besides, I don't think I could eat right now, anyway."

"I think I'll wait with Jennifer," Claire said. "I know what she's going through." Jennifer smiled her thanks.

"All right, but don't you worry, either of you. You'll get your stuff back." Mercedes gave her friends a warm smile. "Take care."

The other four of them went to change and then around to the parking lot. There, Buck and Ned were waiting in the red Jeep. Frank and Joe had joined them, too. Buck's ten-gallon hat was jammed over his forehead, right down to his sunglasses. "Let's go!" he called out. "I'm starving!"

Frank trotted toward the Oldsmobile. "Who wants to come in the White Bird?" he offered.

"Good luck starting it," Ned said.

Frank smiled confidently. "You just don't have the knack, Nickerson."

Joe, Bess, and George followed Frank while Mercedes and Nancy got into the Jeep. Nancy slid in the backseat with Ned, grabbed his hand, and said, "Hi."

"Last one to Port Isabel gets to pay the bill!" Buck shouted.

With a squeal of tires, both cars tore out into the street. Buck had asked to drive, since he knew the way. He pulled ahead and headed toward the causeway to the mainland.

"Where are we going?" Nancy asked.

"Tommy Tulane's Cajun Restaurant," Buck said. "It has the most incredibly huge menu you ever saw! You sit out on a bay while you eat, and there are these singing waiters. . . ."

As Buck rambled on Nancy gazed out the window. The Jeep was on the causeway now, a narrow highway that spanned the Laguna Madre, which separated the mainland from South Padre. Nancy couldn't help but marvel at the light show the setting sun was making on the expanse of turquoise blue water that stretched beneath them in both directions.

The roar of an engine caught her attention. She looked to her left to see a white cigarette boat, fire-red from the sun sitting right on the horizon, racing under the causeway.

"Slow down, Buck!" Nancy said. Leaning out the passenger window, she watched the long, sharp nose of the boat emerge from the other side.

"Is it our thieves?" Ned asked anxiously.

Nancy couldn't see the driver's face, only the reflection off his bald head. When he turned to say something to his gray-haired wife, Nancy noticed that his potbelly was straining against the buttons of his Hawaiian shirt.

"I don't think so," she said with a laugh, watching the boat disappear up the lagoon. To the left of it, a small wooden fishing vessel rocked precariously from its wake. "Those things really are a nuisance, aren't they?"

Suddenly there was a flash of light, then a sharp explosion in the distance, and another directly beneath them. Nancy felt her head jerk violently to the left. A horrifying screech came from the Jeep's tires as Buck jammed on the brakes.

He let out a helpless yell as he yanked the steering wheel to the right and left. The Jeep swerved, out of control.

"Buck!" Mercedes shrieked, trying to grab the steering wheel.

Nancy looked out the window and froze.

Looming toward them at breakneck speed was a short metal fence—the only barrier separating them from the thirty-foot drop to the water below!

Chapter

Nine

NANCY CLOSED HER EYES and reached for Ned's hand. This was it; she knew it. Soon the impact with the water would feel as if they'd hit a stone wall. She gritted her teeth and waited for the crash.

She felt a jolt and heard the crunching of metal. Then she realized the Jeep had stopped moving.

"Nancy," she heard Ned say softly.

Her eyes flew open. "Wh-what?"

Ned gestured for her to look out the window. Peering in from the driver's seat of the White Bird was the ashen face of Frank Hardy.

"It worked," Frank said, amazed.

George looked out from the window behind him. "Amazing," she said.

"Ohhh, I don't believe we're alive!" Bess moaned from the seat next to George.

Mercedes lifted herself from the floor beside Buck. "What happened?"

Nancy could see the dented front fender of the Jeep. She assumed there was a flat tire, because the Jeep was slanting to the right. But she couldn't see the tire, or anything much below the window, because the White Bird was smack up against the Jeep.

"He wedged his car between us and the metal fence," Nancy said.

"It was my idea!" Joe interjected, poking his head over Frank's shoulder.

Buck gave the brothers a wan smile. "Thanks, guys. I don't know what happened."

Nancy suddenly remembered what she had seen and heard just before the Jeep lost control: a flash of light and two explosions.

"I do," Nancy said. She gave Buck a level glance. "We were shot at, Buck."

"What?" came a chorus of voices around her.

"It was someone on that fishing boat in the lagoon!"

Ned pushed open the left-hand door of the Jeep. They all rushed out to look over the railing.

Racing toward the horizon, the boat was far out of reach.

A police siren's high-pitched wail made them all turn around. Weaving around the traffic that had just backed up, a patrol car pulled up behind the two cars.

"What's the problem here?" A burly policeman wearing the name tag Sergeant P. Claiborne hopped out of his cruiser. "I could hear the crash all the way from the main road—"

"Someone shot at us, Officer!" Bess blurted out.

"Uh-huh," Sergeant Claiborne said skeptically. "From another car?"

"From a fishing boat!" George answered.

"A fishing boat," Sergeant Claiborne repeated, raising an eyebrow.

"It's true, Officer," Joe said. "We saw it clearly. The boat raced away up the lagoon, too fast for us to read any markings on it."

"Uh-huh." Sergeant Claiborne made a quick note on his pad, then said, "Okay, let me take your license numbers for the police report. You kids need a tow truck?"

Buck and Frank handed him their licenses, then went to their cars. Since the Jeep was on the left, Buck could jump right in. It was still running, and when he threw it into first it rolled forward. "Nope," he called out the window. "There's a gas station just over the bridge. I can drive there slowly on this tire."

Before Frank could squeeze behind the steering wheel of the White Bird, car horns began to blare all around them. Nancy turned to see traffic pileups leading in both directions to the main roads.

Sergeant Claiborne gave Buck both licenses. "Okay, I'll file a report. Now, clear off this causeway before someone *really* takes a shot at you." He strolled back toward his cruiser.

"Wait a minute!" Ned said. "You don't believe us—"

"To tell the truth, son," Sergeant Claiborne said, settling into the patrol car, "we're a little shorthanded these days—what with all the spring vacation kids and these robberies. But I'll keep my eyes open for an armed fishing boat. That's all I can do." He chuckled as he began to pull around them into the traffic. "And don't forget, a punctured tire sounds an awful lot like a gunshot—"

"Yeah, thanks," Buck mumbled, watching the car edge away, light flashing. "For nothing."

"Forget it," Nancy said. "We'd better clear the road."

Buck got into the driver's seat with Mercedes

beside him. Ned and Nancy clambered into the backseat.

As Buck pulled slowly ahead Nancy heard the White Bird's engine cough and die. Frank tried it a second time. It made a pathetic, whiny noise and died again.

"What was that we said about not needing a tow truck?" Nancy said.

Finally, after four tries, the engine turned over and engaged. Frank caught up to the Jeep and followed slowly, his hazard lights flashing.

They dropped the Jeep off at a gas station but were told they couldn't get it until the next day because the whole rim had to be replaced. They all piled into the White Bird and drove to Tommy Tulane's Restaurant.

The sound of raucous Louisiana Cajun music bounced off the bright walls, which were painted with scenes of New Orleans. Nancy and her friends sat at a round table, riffled through a menu, and quickly ordered their food. As soon as the waiter left Nancy leaned forward over the table. "I found something out. Remember when Rupert Cranston told us about his strange animal collections? What he *didn't* tell us was that one of them was a colony of Portuguese men-of-war— and for some strange reason, he no longer has them."

Silence hung over the table. Frank broke it. "Are you saying what I'm thinking?"

"The jellyfish attack, Buck's jet ski that *happened* to be jammed, the sniper . . ." Nancy scanned the faces at the table. "I wasn't positive until now, but it does look like someone is after Buck."

Buck's face lit up. "Yeah? Like in a TV show?"

Bess and Mercedes laughed.

"This could be serious," Frank said. "Any idea who it might be, Buck? Anyone who might have a grudge against your father? Mr. Cranston?"

"Abe Quinones *does* have a shop near the causeway," Nancy said. "Maybe the boat was his—"

Buck bellowed with laughter. "Come on, guys. This is ridiculous. Nobody would want to *kill* me. All that stuff that happened with my dad is far in the past, and *I* had nothing to do with it. Besides, even if I did, why would they wait till now to get revenge?"

Joe shrugged. "Maybe you did something recently, saw something you weren't supposed to see—"

"Like a body." Nancy's comment fell like a dead weight.

"Great." Frank sighed. "Plenty of leads to follow on that one."

"You guys are *morose*," Buck said. "We Texans ain't into all this gloom and doom. How's about I treat y'all to a big bonfire at the beach after we finish? I know a nice, secluded spot."

Nancy forced a smile. "Sounds great, Buck."

"Speaking of bonfires," George said, "look what's coming."

The sight of a tray full of steaming, spicy Cajun food was enough to stop all detective conversation for the rest of the dinner.

By the time they were all gathered on the beach, Frank felt rested and rejuvenated, the warm Gulf breeze a soothing massage. In a clearing between two sand dunes, he had helped Buck and Joe construct a huge fire. The others were huddled on a blanket—Ned and Nancy with their arms around each other, Mercedes and Bess and George singing softly.

The flames were dancing high in the air. Everyone's face glowed amber in the soft light, and when the girls began harmonizing on an old folk song, Frank closed his eyes and relaxed with the music.

When he opened them, something had changed. About fifty feet away, just beyond a sand dune to their left, there was a gleam of metal. Frank felt a sharp disappointment that someone else had discovered their spot. Maybe they would go away when they realized the spot was taken.

But they didn't. In the light of a full moon, Frank could see the outline of a dune buggy quietly rolling to a stop. He squinted, trying to see the driver.

The buggy started up again. Silently it rolled down the dune and out of sight. Frank kept his eyes trained on the spot where the buggy had disappeared. Sure enough, two shadowy figures appeared over the edge of a closer dune, one of them carrying a long metal object—a shotgun!

Beside him, Nancy had stood to help Joe and Ned toss more driftwood on the fire. The others continued to sing, Buck's rich baritone a lush accent to the sopranos.

Frank leaned over to Nancy, Joe, and Ned. "Don't make a big deal, guys, but there are two people stalking us—with a gun."

With professional calm, the other three glanced at the dune and back.

"Terrific!" Joe said. "We're out in the open—with no place to hide. Buck is history if they come near enough to see us."

"Ssh," Frank admonished. "Don't let the

others know yet. If they panic, those two guys will come running."

Frank's eyes darted over to Buck's ten-gallon hat, which lay neglected on the sand. "Maybe we can sidetrack them." He nonchalantly grabbed the hat and put it on his head. "The parking lot's behind us. Maybe I can get there and into the car before they can get across the sand. I hope they'll tail me, thinking I'm Buck. The rest of you sit tight. When I'm out of sight, tell the others what's happening, then go into town on foot."

He pulled the hat low and dashed into the open, crouching near to the sand.

"Frank, this is crazy!" Nancy called out, running after him. She held out her hand to signal Ned to stay with the others.

Together they broke for the parking lot, running in a frantic zigzag pattern. A shot pinged through the night air.

"What are you doing?" Frank shouted.

"Don't worry!" Nancy said. "We're too far away for a good shot!"

In minutes they reached the parking lot. Frank glanced around; no one was in sight.

"Maybe we lost them," Nancy said, opening the passenger door.

"Don't count on it," Frank replied. He jumped

into the driver's seat and turned on the ignition.

The White Bird made a wheezing noise, then fell silent.

"I don't believe this," Frank said. He tried it again.

This time the car gave two coughs and a shudder.

"You lousy old tank!" He smacked the steering wheel in frustration, then turned the key again.

This time the car roared to life. Frank floored the gas pedal and tore off toward the only exit.

But racing toward them through the exit was a low, dark outline. "Frank, it's them!" Nancy yelled. "They're heading us off!"

Frank slammed his foot on the brake. The gravel beneath them gave way with a clatter as the car spun around.

"How's this thing on sand?" Nancy asked.

Frank gritted his teeth. "Guess we have to find out!"

The White Bird sped out of the parking lot and onto the beach. Frank downshifted as they reached the sand.

A complaining roar came from under the hood. The White Bird skidded across the sand, its rear end swinging wildly.

Behind them, Frank heard the powerful engine

of the dune buggy. As the sound got louder the White Bird struggled ahead, slower and slower.

Suddenly they felt the glare of high beams right on them.

Then the White Bird sank into the sand and stopped!

"We're dead," was all Frank could say.

Chapter

Ten

G ET OUT!" Nancy yelled.

As Frank reached for his door handle Nancy burst out of the passenger door and ran for the nearest dune. The sand slowed her down. Panting, she dived over the crest and rolled down the side. Sand flew into her face and hair. She felt its grittiness in her mouth.

It wasn't until she got to the bottom that she realized Frank wasn't with her.

She scrambled up the side of the dune, sliding back each time the loose sand gave under her. Peering over the top, she saw the dune buggy's taillights bouncing wildly, heading away from her.

Frank must have run the other way, she thought. Judging from the pattern of the taillights, he was leading the sniper in and out of the dunes.

Nancy ran as fast as she could across the thirty feet separating her and the buggy. If she could divert the driver's attention, Frank might be able to escape.

Within seconds, she was close enough to smell the exhaust of the overworked engine. "My foot!" she called out in as deep a voice as she could.

The buggy stopped and began turning. Nancy crouched down and ducked behind a small dune covered with beach grass.

She heard the buggy roar around her on the right. The plan was working. All she had to do was keep out of sight long enough so that the driver wouldn't know it wasn't Buck.

She ran the other way. The buggy followed her, casting ghostly flickers of light over the sand in front of her. A wave of panic gripped Nancy. He had to know she was too small to be Buck. Maybe he was after her, too! She dug her heels in and tried to sprint to the top of a gradual incline and—

"Oof!" This time she really did twist her ankle. She clutched it and tumbled over the top of the dune. Through eyes narrowed with pain, she looked up. She'd tripped over a fence. A wooden slat fence used to prevent erosion. It had been submerged in drifting sand—except for about four inches that jutted from the top of the mound!

Nancy tried to stand, but her leg crumpled beneath her.

It was too late, anyway. The headlight beams caught her square in the face, blinding her. Nancy shielded her eyes and cringed.

The buggy stopped. Nancy tried to roll away from the path of the headlights.

She could hear the driver suddenly shift gears. She looked up to see the buggy backing up. The driver had finally realized he'd been fooled.

With another roar of the engine, the buggy lurched forward again—and drove away. Nancy strained to see the driver, but his face was in shadow from the hood of a sweatshirt.

Shivering with relief, Nancy massaged her ankle. It wasn't broken, just sprained. She struggled to her feet.

She had to find Frank—or at least make sure he had escaped. The buggy seemed to be driving around aimlessly. That was a good sign.

She watched in horror as the buggy stopped about fifty yards away. Then Nancy froze at the sharp crack of a rifle shot. Then the buggy sped away again, farther down the beach.

Her ankle throbbing, Nancy walked as fast as she could to the spot the buggy had just left.

As she got closer she felt her heart sink. Sprawled out on the sand, the ten-gallon hat covering his face, was Frank!

"No!" she screamed. She ran toward him, ignoring the pain in her foot. Tears welled up in her eyes.

"Hey!"

Nancy spun around at the whispered voice. A guy wearing only a bathing suit was running toward her. Behind him, the surf crashed against the sand. Was this a witness?

"It's me, Frank!"

Nancy gasped. "Frank! What are you doing? Who—"

He rushed over to the body. "Not bad, huh?" he said. He grabbed the pants and yanked them off the ground. Sand streamed out of the legs. "Looks like a human, doesn't it? I can't believe they fell for it. What did they think I was doing, sunbathing?"

"You—you scared me," Nancy said feebly. She was torn between the urge to hug him, yell at him, and laugh out loud.

"Oh. Sorry," Frank said with a smile. "I have

you to thank, though. If you hadn't distracted those guys, I wouldn't have been able to make this decoy." He knelt down and pulled up the shirt, which had also been filled with sand. Holding it up to the moon, he looked through a ragged hole in one of the front pockets. "Good shot. Those guys don't mess around."

Frank gathered up the ten-gallon hat, the socks, and the shoes. "I'm freezing," he said. "Let me put these on, then we'll look for the White Bird and try to get out of here."

Nancy followed Frank between two steep dunes. "I don't hear them anymore," he said, changing into his clothes. "You know, I think my trick really did throw them off!"

"Don't be so sure. They may be coming back, or sneaking around on foot—"

"Ssh!"

Nancy fell silent. Frank was looking up at the top of the dune behind her.

Suddenly he flinched. A beam of light flooded him from head to waist.

Nancy glanced over her shoulder.

Slowly a tall, powerful-looking figure descended the sand dune, training his flashlight directly on Frank!

Chapter

Eleven

FRANK GRABBED NANCY'S ARM. "Come on!"

Hand in hand, they ran away from the dune.

"Hey! What's going on here?" the stranger asked.

Nancy whirled around at the sound of the voice. "Ned!" she blurted out.

Ned shone the flashlight on Nancy's face, then Frank's. "Yes, it's me. I had to follow you. Sorry I didn't get here sooner."

Nancy ran over and grabbed him in a giant bear hug.

"Thanks a lot, buddy," Frank said with a smile.

* * *

The next morning at the beach, no one could figure out what had happened at the bonfire. Every theory seemed to fall flat for lack of evidence. Frustrated, Nancy suggested they work on their other problem—the robberies.

Frank began drawing a crude map of the beachfront in the sand. "You know, we *might* be able to trap them," he said. "All of the robberies I've heard about have occurred during the day between eleven and four, and they seem to be moving from south to north—"

"Whoa! Who is *that?*" Joe shielded his eyes from the sun's glare and watched a red-haired girl running along the beach in a bikini. With a broad grin, she waved enthusiastically.

"Steady, Joe," George said.

"I think I'm in heaven," Joe said. "Across the crowded beach, teeming with humanity, the beautiful stranger spots me!"

"Yeah," Mercedes said flatly. "And me and Buck and Frank and Nancy and Bess and George . . . I hate to burst the bubble, Joe, but that's Taryn Quinn. Remember? Our waitress at Dos Banditos."

Bess smiled. "The one with that sensational necklace!"

"Uh-oh," Joe said. "We did leave a tip, didn't we?"

Nancy watched Taryn jog toward them. As she got closer she slowed down, then suddenly stopped. Ripping off her sunglasses, she gave them an odd stare.

"It's us, all right, Taryn!" Mercedes called out.

Taryn smiled abruptly. "Oh, I'm glad you said that. I tell you, without my contact lenses, I am blind as a bat!"

She jogged up to them and sat at the edge of a blanket, sidling up to Frank. "So, y'all, how's your vacation going?"

Her question was met with bemused silence. No one knew quite how to answer.

"Don't all speak at once," Taryn said. Her eyes caught Frank's diagram in the sand. "Ooh, are you an *artist* or something?"

Watching Taryn's coy smile, Nancy bristled a little. She didn't mean to. She knew she had no right to feel insulted—after all, Frank wasn't her boyfriend. He had a girl—a lovely girl—Callie Shaw.

You don't care, Nancy told herself. If Frank wants to flirt, he has every right to.

Frank was grinning modestly. "No, not really. It's a diagram of the beachfront condo complexes. I think we told you about the theft at Buck's place—"

"Right. Your brother's valuables. I remember."

Nancy could see Joe stiffen slightly. She could tell he didn't like being called "your brother" by someone as pretty as Taryn.

"Well, there have been a few more burglaries since then," Frank continued. "Claire's place, and Mercedes's neighbor, Jennifer. The police took reports, but they didn't seem too hopeful."

Taryn's expression melted with concern. "I can't *believe* it. It's like organized crime or something."

Oh, stop trying so hard, Nancy wanted to say.

"It's organized, all right," Mercedes added. "They break into places where a lot of people are staying, so they must know everyone's schedule."

"I wonder what they do with the jewelry," Taryn said.

"Sell it, probably," Nancy shot back. She immediately wished she hadn't said that so sharply. It sounded as if she were trying to imply that Taryn was stupid.

Taryn furrowed her brow. "Hmm, maybe *that's* how Ed Dougherty gets his jewelry."

Mercedes's eyes sprang open. "Ed Dougherty! The guy with the van—I didn't think of him!"

Taryn shrugged. "I know he buys stuff from the

kids around here—but it's mostly things they don't want. You know, old earrings and necklaces that have gone out of style." She smiled. "Then he adds it all to his collection of junk and brings his van out to the beach. You should go see the stuff he tries to sell—secondhand souvenirs, junky little trinkets he makes from seashells. And the tourists just eat it up."

"Once in a while he has a really nice piece of jewelry," Mercedes added. "And whenever you ask him where he got it, he just laughs and says, 'It fell off the back of a truck.'"

"I wouldn't mind checking him out," Bess said.

Claire nudged her and gave a little sneer. "No way, Bess. It's *really* tacky—"

"But it's a good lead." Nancy looked from Joe to Frank. "Our cigarette-boat friends may be feeding this guy—and he doesn't seem to be the type who'd turn them in."

"Do you know where he is, Taryn?" Frank asked.

Taryn thought for a moment, then her eyes lit up. "Yes, I saw him while I was jogging—way up north beyond the hotels. He was hunting for shells."

"How will we find him?" Joe pressed.

"You can't miss his purple van. It's maybe a quarter of a mile past the last hotel."

Frank smiled back at her. "Fantastic, Taryn. Thanks!"

"The Jeep'll go on sand," Buck said. "I'll drive—if it's okay, Mercedes." She nodded her agreement. They had picked the Jeep up that morning.

Buck and Frank ran off, followed closely by Ned and Joe.

"Good luck." Taryn's voice oozed insincerity as she looked at Nancy.

Was that supposed to be some sort of innuendo? Nancy thought. Does she think we're in a contest or something? How dare she think that I'm interested in Frank.

Nancy wanted to laugh it off, to pretend that she didn't catch Taryn's double meaning at all. She smiled as sweetly as she could.

But when she said, "Same to you," she was shocked at the hostility in her voice.

So were Bess and George. They stared at Nancy curiously.

Without saying another word, Nancy ran for the parking lot, too.

Soon they were way past the last hotel and bouncing along the beach.

"Look!" Joe said, hanging out the side of the jeep. "It isn't two different vans after all."

Nancy craned her neck. They had been following two sets of tire tracks. Taryn's "quarter mile past the last hotel" was more like a mile and a half. Worst of all, Joe was right. The two sets of tracks were actually one set. A van had turned around in a semicircle and gone back the way it had come.

"Guess we missed him," Buck said, turning the steering wheel.

"Maybe we can look him up in the phone book," Ned suggested.

Nancy settled back in her seat—then sat bolt upright. "Wait!" she said. Buck slammed on the brakes. Nancy squinted off to the left, where a small area between sand dunes was giving off little metallic glimmers in the sun. "It looks like he dumped some of his stuff over there."

Before she finished her sentence, Joe had hopped out of the Jeep and Buck was driving along behind him.

"This must be the stuff he doesn't want," Joe called out. They all jumped out and knelt over the pile.

It was mostly costume jewelry—cheap bracelets, unmatched earrings, broken necklaces—but there were a few other things thrown in, too.

Like sets of keys.

Joe rummaged through, tossing aside trinkets. Nancy combed through the jewelry with Frank and Ned. And Buck, following a trail of dropped junk, wandered off into the dunes.

Before long, it became clear to Nancy that there was nothing of even the tiniest value there. "I don't know, guys," she said. "We're still going to have to find him. Any luck, Joe?"

"Nah," Joe answered dejectedly. "Maybe he's selling Iola's keys as some kind of sculpture—"

"Hey, look at this!" They all turned at the distant sound of Buck's voice. "We hit the jackpot!"

Sand sprayed left and right as they ran among the dunes. When they tracked Buck down, he was holding a stone about the size of a hardcover book. His eyes were burning with excitement. "Look!" he said.

Joe took the stone and turned it over a couple of times. "Don't tell me—it's kryptonite."

"Look closer," Buck insisted. "On the flat side."

Nancy huddled over the stone. Sure enough, scratched dully into the stone was a partial message: DIG DE—.

The rest of the second word was broken off. "This is it!" Joe exclaimed, falling to his knees.

"What are you talking about?" Ned asked.

"Remember what Roy told us?" Joe replied, his voice charged with excitement. "You know, about the marker for Jean Laffite's treasure?"

The corners of Ned's mouth turned up. "A stone—"

"With the words *Dig Deeper* carved into it!" Buck shouted. He pointed to a depression in the sand. "I found it right there!"

Furiously, they all dug into the sand. In no time they had made a hole about six feet in diameter and a foot deep—but no treasure.

"I don't know about this," Nancy finally said.

"You're not giving up already, are you?" Buck asked incredulously.

"Well, this stone could have washed up from anywhere. And if there *is* a treasure, it's probably halfway to China. I mean, these guys probably used shovels, right? And here we are with our bare hands—"

"I got it!" Joe yelled.

Frantically everyone helped him dig around a curved, dull metallic object.

"It's too small to be a chest," Ned said, scraping around the basketball-size object.

"And it sure ain't a necklace," Buck commented.

"Then what is it?" Nancy asked.

Suddenly Joe pulled his hand away. The color had drained from his face. "It's an artillery shell!" he said. "This thing is about to go off in our faces!"

Chapter

Twelve

"GET THEM AWAY, JOE!" Frank shouted. "I'll delay the fuse!"

"You'll be killed, Frank!" Nancy said.

Joe pulled her by the arm. "He knows what he's doing. Come on!"

Frank's neck muscles were stiff with tension. Sweat was forming in a warm pool around his collar. His hands brushed aside the sand, revealing a little tube of mercury fulminate—the detonator. All he needed to do was rip it out—but gently. One jiggle of the shell and it was all over. He hooked his fingers delicately under it.

Suddenly he felt a hand on his shoulder. "Are you crazy?" It was Buck.

"Buck, no!" Frank yelled.

He tried to let go of the detonator, but it was

too late. As Buck pulled him backward he couldn't help yanking on the shell.

Panic ripped through him. "Hit the ground!"

They did. Frank wrapped his arms over his head. He felt foolish and vulnerable—nothing he could do would protect him from the explosion. . . .

At least there was *supposed* to be an explosion. Nothing happened. Frank looked behind him. The shell was closer than he realized, and the detonator was peeking up out of the sand. A little dark mass was bubbling through the sand caked around the glass tube. Then it dripped onto the ground.

Frank couldn't believe it. Sand was jamming the detonator!

"Is everything okay now?" Buck asked.

"Don't ask questions," Frank shot back. "Run!"

They took off across the sand. Frank looked up to see the others, just beyond Mercedes's Jeep, looking anxiously back—

When the explosion finally came, Frank was hurtled forward, head over heels. With a whack he landed against the side of the Jeep. The ground vibrated beneath him like a rumbling subway train. He shielded his face as sand rained down around him.

Then, as suddenly as the explosion had occurred, there was silence. Frank took his arm away from his face—that meant it was still attached. He sat up slowly. Both legs were there. . . . He could move his toes. . . .

"You all right?"

Frank spun around to see Buck leaning over him. His clothes were dusty with sand, his hair in strands across his face. "You're—alive!" Frank said.

"Thanks to you," Buck returned. "How did you delay the fuse?"

"Me? *I* didn't—" Frank began. But he didn't have time to finish.

"Frank! You did it!" Nancy shouted, rushing up to him.

Ned was right behind her. "We owe our lives to you, buddy," he said with an admiring grin.

Joe's face was glowing with pride. Without saying a word, he clapped his brother on the back.

Frank exhaled. He could tell them the truth later. Right then he felt too good to do anything but smile.

On the way home after dropping off Frank, Joe, and Ned, Nancy felt as if she were in a hearse, not a Jeep. Buck was angry and refused to talk to her, refused even to acknowledge she was in the car. Frank and Joe had ordered him to go straight home while they and Ned investigated the explosion.

"Cool breeze today," Nancy said cheerfully.

"Mm-hm." Buck stared straight ahead.

As he drove the Jeep onto the main road Nancy drummed her fingers on her knee. If only he weren't so angry . . .

"Oh, Buck," she finally said, with an exasperated sigh. "Don't you understand? Frank and Joe are concerned about your safety. They just want you to be out of harm's way!"

"I know," Buck said, his jaw set. "But what *you* all don't understand is that I'm fed up with this garbage. It's *me* these guys are after. I don't know who they are, but I want them. I want them bad." He slammed the steering wheel. "And I can't find them if I'm being quarantined!"

Nancy had to hold back a giggle. His anger was kind of funny. It didn't really fit his happy-go-lucky personality.

"You're laughing," he said, astonished.

Nancy pulled her face muscles tight. "No, I'm not."

"You are."

"I'm not."

Out of the corner of her eye, Nancy could see the edges of Buck's mouth creeping upward. She couldn't help bursting into laughter.

"I told you!" Buck said.

"All right, all right! You win!"

Nancy had decided to go home with Buck and then drive Mercedes's Jeep back to her condo. He parked in a secluded corner, under the shadow of a huge palm. And when Nancy reached for her door handle, he grabbed her left hand.

Startled, Nancy turned to face him. He was staring at her with a penetrating look that gave her a small shiver.

She managed a polite smile, keeping her right hand on the door. "Uh, Buck," she said, "why don't we——"

"I have an idea!" he interrupted.

"Huh?"

"I know a way we can get these snipers. It's perfect!"

Nancy felt relief wash over her. "Oh, great!"

He looked over his shoulder and scanned the parking lot. Then he whispered, "Maybe we should go inside. You never know if you're being spied on."

"Right, Buck."

They left the Jeep and walked into the condo.

Buck's eyes darted left and right, as if someone was about to jump out of the walls at him.

He unlocked the front door and ushered Nancy inside. Following her, he slammed the door shut. "Whew, we made it!" he said. "Stay here."

He scampered around the apartment, checking each room.

"We're safe," he finally called out from the second floor.

"What a relief," Nancy replied. She was getting a kick out of this. Instead of being afraid for his life, Buck thought he was in some sort of cloak-and-dagger adventure.

"Anyway, you want to hear my plan?" he asked, bounding down the stairs.

"Sure."

"We set me up as a target," he said enthusiastically, as if he had just unearthed the most brilliant plan in the universe. "And then we can lure them out!"

Nancy waited for the rest of it, the details. But he just stared at her expectantly. "That's it?" Nancy replied.

"Brilliant, huh?"

"I don't know, Buck—"

"Oh, come on! You guys expect me to just sit around while you grab all the glory?"

"No, it's just that we have to wait until Frank and Joe investigate the bomb site, then we have to discuss a strategy when they get back. It's the only way you can come up with something really specific—"

"I can be specific—"

Nancy was glad the phone cut him off. He snatched the receiver off the hook. "Hello . . . Oh, hi, Mercedes. You won't believe what just happened—what? . . . You do? What is it? . . . Oh, right . . . Okay, great . . . 'Bye."

"What did Mercedes want?" Nancy asked.

"She says she has important news about the case, but she didn't want to talk on the phone, so she's getting a ride over with a friend. Are you hungry?" Nancy nodded. "I'm starved. Let's eat first, and then I'll tell you about my idea."

After they had a sandwich, Buck launched into his plan. "We could go to Dos Banditos, right? Then we could eat at different tables, and then I could go for a walk by myself at night on the beach, and then you could—"

"Buck," Nancy interrupted with a gentle smile, trying to put the plan to rest. "Who knows, your idea might be smarter than anything we come up with. I'll mention it to the others, okay?"

Buck's face broke into a radiant smile. "All

right, I knew you would!" He wrapped his arms around her and lifted her into the air with a big bear hug. "You are one sensational woman!"

Just then Nancy heard the door creak behind her. With dread, she realized they'd forgotten to close it. Still locked in Buck's embrace, she turned her head.

And came face-to-face with Mercedes.

Buck released Nancy. "Hey, that was quick!" he said jovially to Mercedes.

"Yeah, *too* quick, I see!" she said, her face pale and her eyes filled with hurt.

"Mercedes, I—" Nancy began to explain.

But it was too late. Mercedes had turned on her heel and stormed out, slamming the door behind her.

Chapter

Thirteen

WHAT'S HER PROBLEM?" Buck said.

"Oh, Buck. Can't you see?" It was hard not to like Buck, she thought, but sometimes he was a little dense.

Nancy ran to the door and opened it. Outside, the beach was crowded. Mercedes could have gone anywhere. Nancy started running down the beach to the right, in the general direction of Mercedes's place. But it was fruitless; she was nowhere to be seen.

Nancy trudged back, walking around a limbo contest, where a guy with a Sigma Chi T-shirt was bent backward, trying to crawl under a stick. His friends were shouting encouragement, as if it were the most important thing in the world to them.

Must be nice, Nancy thought. Right then she really felt as if she *were* in limbo. Her mind was reeling—now she had to solve an attempted murder, solve a series of burglaries, and patch up a huge misunderstanding with an old friend.

In less than one week.

When she got back to Buck's condo, she cheered up a bit. Ned was at the front door.

"Wow, am I glad you're back!" she cried out.

"Hi," Ned answered in a subdued voice.

"Is everything all right?" she asked. "Where are Frank and Joe?"

"Frank's out on the beach with that waitress from Dos Banditos. We stopped to talk to her and Mercedes on the way here. Joe's inside with Buck."

"Oh?" Nancy said. Suddenly she realized why Ned was so quiet. "Did you talk to Mercedes?"

Ned nodded. "Yep. She was pretty upset. She said she saw you and Buck in a—what did she call it?—a compromising position. . . ."

"What?" Nancy laughed. "He was just hugging me, that's all."

"Hugging you?"

"Not romantically or anything. He was just

being happy. Mercedes was jumping to conclusions."

"Uh-huh."

"Oh, Ned. You don't really believe that Buck would—"

Ned's eyes narrowed. "It's not so unbelievable, Nancy. I mean, he's admitted he has a crush on you, he's dying to be alone with you, and then I'm stupid enough to let it happen. I can't believe how naïve I was!"

"What do you mean, *let* it happen?"

"You know what I mean. If I hadn't said okay when Frank and Joe suggested you take Buck back—"

"I can't believe you're saying this, Ned." Nancy folded her arms. "This doesn't sound like you. What are you implying? That I had no say in it? That you control every move I make?"

"Oh, so you *wanted* to be alone with Buck? Is that what *you're* saying? That it was your idea?"

"No! I mean, yes! I mean, that's not the point!"

Ned threw up his arms. "Fine. When you make up your mind, Nancy, just let me know, okay?"

With that he turned and left.

Nancy started to chase after him, then held herself back. What was the use? They'd only continue yelling at each other. Maybe it would be better to let the whole thing blow over.

She reached for the doorknob. Then, from behind the door, she caught the sound of a baseball game on TV and loud cheering from Joe and Buck.

Obviously it wasn't necessary for her to be looking after Buck now—which was just fine. Seeing Buck was the last thing she wanted to do.

Besides talking to Ned.

Maybe she could find Bess and George— they'd help her sort things out. She took a long walk down the beach to cool off. Eventually she stopped near the white lifeguard stand, where she hoped Claire and Bess would be hanging out.

"Hey, Drew!" she heard a voice call out.

She turned and looked all around for Frank. When she didn't see him, she looked down. There, ten feet away, was Frank's head. The rest of him was buried under the sand. She smiled, amazed at how quickly he'd recovered from the shock of that explosion.

Her smile disappeared when she saw Taryn hovering over him, packing the sand down tightly with her feet.

"You'll never get a tan that way," Nancy said.

"But I'll have the face of a bronze god," Frank replied.

Taryn gave a glance over her shoulder to

Nancy, smiled briefly, then said, "Well, that's all right with me. I have a thing for bronze gods."

Taryn couldn't really believe Frank would fall for a stupid line like that, thought Nancy.

But Frank was beaming. "You'd better watch it, Tarry, before I strike you down with one of my thunderbolts."

He's got to be kidding, Nancy thought. He must be making fun of her. It's a private joke, meant for me to recognize.

She looked at Frank for some sort of conspiratorial look, a nod, a wink . . . *anything.*

No such luck. His eyes were following Taryn's every move.

Suddenly Nancy felt indignant. "Frank, you have a—" *Girlfriend* was the word she wanted to use, but she stopped herself. It was none of her business bringing Callie Shaw into this. Frank could manage his own life, after all. . . .

"Frank has a what, Nancy?" Taryn asked in a slightly too-sweet voice.

"A sunburn," Nancy said quickly. "Be careful. See you later."

"'Bye!" Taryn sang, and she went back to work covering Frank.

Dejected and confused, Nancy kept walking. Sure enough, Bess, Claire, and George had staked out their usual spot by the lifeguard stand. "Hi, guys," Nancy said as she approached.

George looked back to see Nancy, then put on a mock-solemn expression. "Hey, don't look so unhappy. I know life in paradise is tough, but we'll be leaving in a few days."

Nancy managed a half smile. "Thanks for the encouragement."

Bess smoothed out a section of blanket and gestured for Nancy to sit. "What's up? Something about the robberies?"

"No," Nancy answered. "That's not what—"

"Guess what? Claire has a police inventory of the things stolen from her and Jennifer's apartments. Show her, Claire."

Claire had already pulled a few sheets out of her shoulder bag. She handed them to Nancy. "Here."

Nancy looked them over. "Jewelry, series EE savings bonds—a lot of the same types of stuff."

"Jennifer's dad and my dad work together," Claire said. "And they've both been making all the same kinds of investments for us."

"Really . . ." Nancy said. Now we're getting somewhere, she thought. "Did you notice anything else about the police list—anything the victims had in common?"

"Not really," Claire answered. "I mean, I know all six of them—one of the girls is a real jock, there's a sort of nerdy guy—"

"Wait a minute," George interrupted. "If you know them all, *that's* something they have in common."

Nancy nodded. "These crooks are well-organized. They're going straight for the portable stuff, they know exactly where it is, and they know who has the goods—"

"And when to break in," Bess said.

Claire looked puzzled. "So if *we* can figure all this out, why didn't the police? When I asked them, they said they couldn't figure out anything from the inventory."

"Maybe they're in on this," George suggested.

"Or maybe they've been told to keep it hush-hush," Nancy said. "The town leaders might not want news of this to get into the press. I mean, it wouldn't be too great for the tourist trade."

Bess stood up. "I think we should tell Frank and Joe right now—either that or go into the water."

Nancy thought of approaching Frank and Taryn again. The thought lasted about two seconds. She pulled off her sweat shirt. "Let's go in the water."

* * *

That evening Nancy had to wait for Ned to pick her, Bess, and George up for dinner. Mercedes—and her Jeep—hadn't shown up all evening. Nancy had a feeling she was off sulking.

But right now her thoughts were centered on Ned. When she'd called him to say that they all needed a ride, his reply was distant. Obviously, he still didn't want to talk to her.

Nancy waved as he pulled up in the White Bird, but only Frank and Joe waved back. Ned remained silent as they all piled in and didn't say a word until Nancy finally suggested, "Why don't we go someplace new for dinner?"

Ned's only reply was, "Frank wants to go to Dos Banditos."

When they got there, Nancy knew exactly why. It was obvious from the look on Frank's face when Taryn came over to deliver the basket of chips. It was a look Nancy recognized—a look she had often gotten from Ned.

But not that night. In fact, he wasn't looking at Nancy at all. But when Taryn left to go back to the kitchen, he gave Frank a knowing grin as if to say, "Not bad!"

You really know how to make a girl feel good, Nickerson, Nancy thought.

She watched everyone's hands plunge into the

chips. Normally she would have joined them, but at that moment she had absolutely no appetite. There was only one thing on her mind.

She had to speak to Ned.

Nancy took a deep breath. She caught an encouraging glance from Bess—*she* could tell what was going on. Then, as calmly as she could, Nancy got up, walked behind Ned, and gently put a hand on his shoulder. "Can we talk?" she murmured in his ear.

Ned looked up. He had a smile on his face, but Nancy could see little muscle tugs near the corners of his eyes that showed he was taken by surprise. "Okay," he replied.

Together they walked outside. The nearly full moon cast a broad streak of orange on the sea. It seemed to follow them as they walked silently on the sand.

"So," Nancy said, "are you talking to me?"

"I guess I am," Ned said with a shrug, "no matter what I answer."

Nancy smiled. "Well, it's a start. Maybe you'll tell me why you were so cold to me today."

Ned rolled his eyes. "Well, what did you expect, Nancy? After what I heard from Mercedes—and then you didn't deny it!"

"Ned, Buck was happy because he'd thought up a way to catch the attempted murderer—making himself the hero, of course. I told him we'd think about it, so he gave me a hug. You know how overexcited he gets sometimes."

Ned looked down at the sand.

"There's nothing between Buck and me," Nancy went on, "and if you had given me a chance, I would have explained that to you."

Ned bent over and tossed a stone into the water. When he looked at Nancy, his expression had softened. "I-I'm sorry, Nancy. I guess I just took Mercedes too seriously. I mean, she was ready to kill."

"I know. She's probably still not over it. We haven't heard from her since—" Nancy stopped short. "What's that, Ned?" She pointed up to the road.

It was an empty red Jeep, parked at a skewed angle on the shoulder with its driver's door hanging open.

Ned squinted. "Is that Mercedes's?"

Without answering, Nancy ran to the Jeep. As she got closer she could make out the license plate. "It's hers, all right," she called over her shoulder.

"Why would she park here? The only thing

around is the restaurant, and she wasn't inside," Ned said.

Nancy peeked into the car. "And why would she leave the keys in the ignition?" She turned to Ned, feeling a sudden knot in her stomach. "Something is definitely not right here."

Chapter

Fourteen

"Mercedes!" Nancy called out for what seemed to be the hundredth time. From farther down the beach, Nancy could hear Ned echo her.

"It's no use," he said, running up. "I've cased the beach all the way to that jetty."

"And I went all the way down past the shops," Nancy replied.

"Did you check inside any of them?"

"A couple. But if she was shopping, she wouldn't have left the car like this. Come on, let's get the others. We've got to find her."

Nancy and Ned sprinted back to Dos Banditos. Taryn was standing beside their table, pad in hand. She threw her head back and laughed at something Frank said.

"Guys," Nancy announced, "we have to go."

Taryn gave her a chilly glance. "Huh?"

"We just ordered appetizers," Frank protested.

"Mercedes is missing," Nancy said. She looked over her shoulder. "You can cancel the order, right, Taryn?"

"Well, I guess—"

Before she could finish, they were all heading for the front door.

First they called Buck, who hadn't seen her. He said he'd pick up Mercedes's Jeep and meet them at her condo. There was always a chance that she had gone home.

"Hello!" Nancy called into the apartment. "Mercedes?"

"She left," a voice came from the top of the stairs.

"Left?" Nancy answered. "When was she here?"

Kristin appeared in her bathrobe. "She ran in a little while ago, but she didn't stay long. She was in a hurry to get to dinner."

"Did she say where she was going?" Frank asked.

The girl was running a brush through her just-washed hair. "Dos Banditos, I think."

"Thanks." He turned to the others. "Somebody must have stopped her on the way."

"Nancy, this is creepy," Bess said. "Let's call the police."

Buck joined them just then. "There's not much else we can do."

With that, they all walked to the kitchen, snaking their way through the living room. Nancy called the police and gave a report.

But their response wasn't what she had wanted, although she did expect it. With a glum expression, she hung up the phone and looked into the expectant faces of her friends. "They can't do anything for forty-eight hours."

"Why not?" Claire asked.

"Standard procedure, they said. Ninety-nine percent of the time the missing person shows up within two days."

"Yeah, but you told him about the abandoned car!"

Nancy shrugged. "They said she might have gone for a walk on the beach."

"That's a big help," George commented.

"How about Mercedes's parents?" Frank suggested, scanning a handwritten list of phone numbers taped to the wall. "Their number's here. She might have called them."

Nancy started to pick up the receiver, but Buck stopped her. "It's a speakerphone," he said. "If you press the speaker button, we can all listen."

Nancy pressed the button marked SPKR and quickly punched in the number.

"Hello?" a singsong voice crackled into the room.

"Hi," Nancy said into the speaker. "Is this Mrs. Cole?"

"Yes."

"This is Nancy Drew. I don't know if you remember—"

"Nancy from summer camp!" Her voice brightened. "Of course I remember. Mercedes is so happy you've gotten together again! And she's told me you've become a private detective."

"Yes, well—"

"How thrilling! Oh, I should have known. You were always so observant."

"Thanks, Mrs. Cole," Nancy said. "Actually, I was wondering if you had heard from Mercedes tonight."

"Not for a couple of days. Isn't she with you?"

Nancy swallowed. "Well, we don't know where she is, Mrs. Cole. I'm sure she's probably out taking a walk or something—"

"That's not like her. She said she was going to spend all of her time with you." Mrs. Cole's voice became agitated. "Do you think something's happened? When did you last see her?"

"This afternoon—"

Mrs. Cole sounded devastated. "Oh, my dear! Where could she be?"

"I didn't mean to scare you, Mrs. Cole. We just want to be on the safe side, that's all."

"Did you call the police?"

"I did. But we're not just going to leave it to them. We're going to search every inch of South Padre—now."

Nancy heard a frantic rustling of paper. "This is terrible. The last flight has left—"

"I know we'll find her," Nancy said reassuringly. "Please don't worry."

"Yes. Yes, of course. . . ." Mrs. Cole's voice drifted off. She exhaled deeply and said in a fragile voice, "You will promise to find her, won't you? I—I feel so helpless here, clear across the state."

"Of course," Nancy said. "I give you my word."

"Thank you, sweetheart. And please call me, all right?"

"All right. Good night, Mrs. Cole."

"Good night."

Nancy pressed the speaker button again, and the phone clicked off. She sighed. "Major mistake. Now she's so upset she won't sleep."

"Well, we better do something," Bess said. "You just gave her your word."

Nancy paced back and forth. "But what? We don't have any leads."

Ned put his arm around her. "You told Mrs. Cole what we'll do—we're going to search every inch of South Padre. But we've got to wait until tomorrow, Nan. We really can't do it at night. She's probably blowing off steam somewhere and will show up tonight."

"Yeah," Nancy said. *"If* she's still okay."

Nancy's eyes popped open as the sun peeked over the horizon. She didn't know how long she'd slept, but it couldn't have been much more than an hour. Every time she had heard a teeny noise she'd jumped up, thinking it was Mercedes. And every time it was nothing—no one.

Beside her, Bess lay peacefully on her side. Nancy nudged her.

"Huh—wha—" Bess mumbled.

"She's not here," Nancy whispered.

Bess sat up, blank-eyed. "Who?"

"Mercedes."

"Oh." Bess slumped back down into her sleeping bag.

"We're going to find her—now. Wake George up, okay? I'll call the guys."

As Bess leaned over to George Nancy stepped into the kitchen, where the boys had spent the night. They wanted to get a jump on the search.

She grimaced at the sight of Frank, Joe, Ned, and Buck curled uncomfortably on blankets spread across the tile floor. At least she didn't feel bad waking them—they'd probably be grateful.

"Good morning," she said softly.

No answer.

"Time to get up, guys."

Still nothing. There had to be some way to rouse them.

"Who wants bacon with their eggs?" she tried.

Joe's eyes flickered. "Ugh, is it morning already?"

Before long the others were up. Groggily, they joined the three girls around the table. "Mercedes didn't come in, did she?" Buck asked softly.

Nancy shook her head. Looking around, she saw that everyone's face was grim with concern. "We're going to have to split into groups to search the island," she said. "This is going to take everyone we can recruit. Let's go to the other condos here and ask for help."

"We can't all leave," Bess said. "What if Mercedes calls?"

"We'll take shifts manning the phones," Frank suggested. "One group will be here at all times."

Later that evening Joe had just hung up the phone in the kitchen. He glanced at the kitchen clock, which said 10:15 P.M. The day had dragged like a week. "That was Nancy," he told Buck. "She and Ned and Frank just finished searching North Padre and didn't find a thing."

Buck paced the kitchen floor impatiently, as if he hadn't heard Joe. "This is a waste," he said. "We don't need *two* people waiting by the phone."

Joe rolled his eyes. Buck had been complaining ever since their phone shift started. "We have to do it this way," Joe said. "If *you* go around alone, you're a sitting duck!"

"But that could be part of the plan—"

Joe was relieved that the telephone's ring saved him from another argument right then.

Buck pressed a button, activating the phone's speaker. "Hello, this is Buck, and I could use some good news."

The silence at the other end was broken only by the screech of a sea gull and the start of a distant motor.

"Hello?" Buck repeated. "Hey, I was only kidding. I'll take any news."

A low chuckle oozed out of the speaker. Joe sat up. "I've got news for you, Buck—*real* good news." The voice was raspy and muffled, as if there was a handkerchief over the phone. But there was something familiar about it to Joe. "Your girlfriend is safe—at least for the time being."

Buck shot a look at Joe, who gestured to him to keep talking. "Uh, what are you getting at?" Buck replied.

"I'm offering you a business proposition, Mr. Buchanan. My office hours are from four A.M. till four-oh-one, at the fishing pier. There's one small condition: You must bring Nancy Drew, and no one else. The trouble is, you have to find me— and if there is anyone else with you besides the Drew girl, you *won't* find me—and you'll be very sorry."

Buck swallowed. "I don't understand. What's the deal?"

"Your girlfriend," the voice said coldly, "for you."

Chapter

Fifteen

THE PHONE CLICKED OFF before Buck could say a word.

Joe stood up from his chair. "Who *was* that? He sounded familiar."

Buck's face was pale. He shook his head slowly. "They're going to kill me—"

"No, they're not!" Joe insisted. "We'll stop them, Buck. But we need help—think about the voice."

"I—I don't know—"

"Then what about the location? Where was he calling from? Obviously it was outdoors."

Buck sank back into his seat, deep in thought. "The motors—they sounded like outboard engines. And the sea gulls meant he was probably near food."

"Some outdoor restaurant?"

"At the all-night pier!" Buck said. "Boats going out, people having late dinner—"

Joe began pacing. "He's there now, and he's staying until four A.M. And he's not afraid of anyone noticing him."

"Maybe he works there," Buck suggested.

"Maybe he owns a shop, like Abe's Bait and Tackle."

Buck looked at Joe as if he were crazy. "Abe Quinones?"

"He and your dad aren't exactly pals, are they?"

"No . . ."

"I say that's the place we check out first at four A.M."

A grin slowly made its way across Buck's face. "Why four A.M.? They'll be looking for us then. I say we go now and rescue Mercedes when they least expect it!"

"It's a good idea," Joe said, "but we can't."

"What are you talking about? We'd be stupid to wait—"

"We'd be stupider to go down there, not knowing for sure who we're looking for. He takes one look at you, and there's no telling how he'll retaliate. We've got to sit tight and wait for Nancy to call. Maybe we can send Ned and Frank—"

Buck's face was set. "Listen, buddy. If you don't want to go down there, I'm going—alone. You know as well as I do, there's no time to lose."

Joe took a deep breath. There was no way he'd let Buck out of his sight. And keeping him at the condo wouldn't be easy. . . .

"Okay," Joe finally said. "Let's go for it."

Winding through the streets of Corpus Christi, Nancy kept her eyes peeled. It was a typical spring-vacation night scene: Groups of teens and college kids were gathered outside all the restaurants, pizza joints, and nightclubs. But there was no sign of Mercedes.

Just as Ned was about to turn back onto the main highway, Frank called out, "Is that her?"

Ned stopped the White Bird outside an ice-cream stand. Nancy had to agree with Frank. The dark-haired girl standing with her back to them had to be Mercedes. She was deep in conversation with two other girls.

"Mercedes?" Frank called out.

One of the girl's friends nudged her, but she didn't turn around.

"Mercedes!"

"Will you leave me alone?" Spinning around, the girl threw back her dark hair, revealing an annoyed frown. "What are you, a car salesman or something?"

"Sorry, I thought you were someone else," Frank said, putting the car in gear. *"Named* Mercedes."

They had looked all over for Mercedes— starting on the South Padre beaches, working their way up into the National Park, creeping around sand dunes. They'd combed the ranger station, two trailer parks, and the medical center, and had driven all the way to join the search team on North Padre. Now they were heading home.

As they sped down the highway, beginning the two-hour drive back to South Padre, Ned said, "We can't be too hard on ourselves. There are eighty miles of wilderness beach between North and South Padre. Who knows? She may be camping out, trying to get away from . . ." His voice trailed off.

"From me," Nancy said matter-of-factly.

Ned didn't respond. Something about his attitude toward Nancy had changed since their confrontation. Sure, they had made up, she thought, but it wasn't the same. There was a distance between them now, an ever-so-slight lack of trust. It made Nancy nervous.

"I just can't help feeling she was kidnapped," Nancy continued. "Maybe by someone who wants to get to Buck."

"I don't know," Frank remarked. "There haven't been any ransom notes or phone calls. The less we hear, the better I feel."

Nancy nodded, fighting back her ugly speculations. What if Buck's snipers hadn't kidnapped Mercedes? Maybe they were angry that Buck had gotten away from them—maybe they were out for revenge, and they were taking it out on Mercedes.

Nancy shuddered. There was only one place they hadn't dared look for Mercedes so far.

The water.

By the time they got to Mercedes's condo, a couple of the search groups had already returned. Nancy wished Bess and George would come back, but they were checking out the late-night clubs.

Ned ran in to answer the ringing phone, while Nancy and Frank collapsed in the living room to compare notes with the others.

The story was the same with everyone. A few

sightings that turned out to be false alarms, a lot of time wasted—

In the middle of a conversation, Ned's voice boomed out into the living room. "Hey, where are Joe and Buck?"

Nancy looked at her watch. "They had the nine-to-one shift. They should still be here."

She and Frank went into the kitchen. There, Ned had just found a note written on a yellow legal pad. Nancy read it over his shoulder:

> Had to run. Whoever gets here first,
> please take over the phone shift.
> Thanks.
> Joe Hardy

Frank was seething. "What the— He knows he's not supposed to do this!"

"Where could they have gone?" Ned asked.

"Knowing those two," Nancy said, "they got bored and went looking for Mercedes."

Frank nodded. "I love my brother," he said, his voice tinged with anger. "But when he gets back, I'm going to let him have it."

Buck and Joe were winding their way around a huge group of college students gathered outside a restaurant. Across the street a couple of beefy guys broke into an ear-splitting, tuneless rendition of their college football fight song.

Then suddenly the whole street erupted with noise—cheers trying to drown out jeers, a chorus of insults going back and forth between kids from rival schools.

Joe peered through the crowd to the end of the block. Above a darkened front window, the Abe's Bait and Tackle sign hung unlit. "It looks closed," he said.

"Strange," Buck replied. "Abe always stays open at night. Says it's the best time for business."

Approaching the store, Joe looked around carefully. There seemed to be no one following them or watching them. He tried the shop's door handle, which was locked tight. There was a Closed sign hanging in the door, and the shop looked tidy inside.

"Is he on vacation?" Joe asked.

"Never during the busy season," Buck said.

Joe looked around the left side of the shop. An alleyway led to a small, dark yard in the back. Lining the far edge of the yard were a cement sidewalk and a dark wooden fence that overlooked a channel to Laguna Madre. A small pier jutted out into the water.

"Let's split up," Buck said. "I'll take the left, you go right."

"Okay. Yell if you get into trouble."

Keeping close to the white-shingled wall, Joe made his way around the shop. Cautiously, he looked into the side windows. A scarred butcher-block table—a storeroom full of fishing rods—two floor-to-ceiling refrigerator cases. No signs of life at all.

At the end of this right alley was a chain-link fence with a locked gate. To get to the yard, Joe would have to climb it.

He clutched the fence and inserted his foot.

"No! Help!"

It was Buck, from the left alleyway. With lightning-quick reflexes, Joe scaled the fence and hopped over. He ran through the overgrown yard, tripping over discarded tackle and bags of spoiled bait, to the left alleyway.

"Leave me—ugh!"

A thud echoed dully from between the buildings. Joe plunged into the pitch-black alley—and was immediately stopped by the viselike grip of two gloved hands around his throat!

Joe drew his arm up and back and swung. He made contact.

"Yeooww!" The hands immediately loosened

from around his neck. Joe toppled forward—and lost his balance.

Something was beneath him. Something soft, heavy, and inert. Something like a body.

He rolled over once and smacked up against the wall of the shop next door. Around him, he heard frantic footsteps and a heavy dragging sound. He stood up.

An object was flying up to meet his face. He jerked his head back and felt only the draft. His eyes had adjusted to the darkness now, and he could tell the object was a foot. A foot belonging to someone short and thin.

Joe quickly glanced down. His eyes traced the silhouette of Buck's crumpled, unconscious body.

But there was something else, too—another body! Joe did a double take. Mercedes?

He was taken unawares by a heavy blow to his right shoulder. Grimacing with pain, he fell to the ground.

In front of him a tall, broad-shouldered person crouched.

"How nice of you to come down to my level," Joe said. He propelled himself forward.

Whirling into motion, the attacker rose from the ground, flinging his arms into Joe.

"Arrrrgh!" Joe felt as if he'd been slapped in

the face. Then something was flying down over his head. And when he tumbled to the ground again, tangled in a taut, thick web, he knew exactly what it was.

A fishing net!

Before he could react, he caught a glancing kick in the head. And for a moment he blacked out.

It couldn't have been more than a few seconds, but when he came to, he felt his legs scraping against scrubby ground.

He looked up. The two assailants were dragging him across the yard. He tried to get up, but it was impossible. The cords of the enormous net dug into him on all sides. "Hey, this is pretty brave, huh?" Joe called out.

No response.

"Who are you twerps anyway?" he tried. Now, as they moved into the dim reflection of some of the lights from the pier, he could tell they were wearing masks. "Which one of you is Abe—hey —HEY!"

Suddenly Joe felt himself being lifted off the ground. He looked down, and his eyes popped open. All he could do was stare in horror as he plunged toward the still, black water of the channel!

Chapter

Sixteen

THE WATER ENGULFED HIM with a loud splash. He tried to flail with his arms and legs, but the net weighed him down and bound him. In seconds he hit bottom. The muck from below oozed into the net, making it even heavier.

Don't panic, Joe, he said to himself. You'll float. And he did; his natural buoyancy lifted him upward as he patiently tried to peel the net from around him.

Bursting above the surface, he gasped for air. The wet strands of the net still covered his face and hands. But his legs were free, so he trod water furiously to keep from sinking.

And that was when he heard the shuffling

noises on the pier. He maneuvered his body around to look.

Moving stealthily in the darkness, the two figures dragged Buck and Mercedes to the edge of the pier. The larger of the two kidnappers then dropped over the edge so that only his upper body showed over the dock.

They had a boat, Joe realized. He'd have to swim around the pier to get to it. With quick, rhythmic movements he pulled sections of the net off his head.

An outboard engine roared. Now both partners—and both bodies—were on the getaway boat.

Time was running out. Frantically treading water, Joe pulled at the last bits of net. Finally he was free. With a surge of energy, Joe swam toward the dock.

He was no more than ten feet away when the boat shot out into the lagoon.

A cigarette boat.

It was impossible to try to follow. Within seconds the boat was out of sight.

Joe floated in the water for a few seconds, then swam to the pier and boosted himself on the dock. Leaving a trail of water, he began the short walk back to Mercedes's condo. He could feel frustration welling up inside—and guilt. Guilt that he had let Buck walk into a trap.

He knew that when he got back, there'd be a lot of explaining to do.

Frank paced the kitchen floor. "I can't believe he didn't write down where they were going."

One of Mercedes's friends passed through and opened the refrigerator. "Maybe they went shopping. There's no food here."

Ned stared dully at the kitchen table. "I'm too tired to eat. I'm too tired to *move.*"

Just then the front door opened. "Yucchhh, what happened to *you?*" came a voice from the living room.

Nancy looked inside. Everyone was staring at Joe, who was soaked from head to toe.

"I took a swim," Joe replied with an innocent shrug. "The water's great at night."

No one said a word as he walked into the kitchen. Frank shut the door behind him. "Okay, what happened?" he demanded.

As Joe told them about his adventure Nancy had a sinking feeling. Joe had foiled the kidnappers' plans—only to make the situation twice as bad. Instead of using Mercedes as a hostage to try to get Buck, the kidnappers now had them both.

Frank bolted up from his chair and grabbed the

phone book. "We've got to track down Qui-nones!"

The telephone ring was like an electric shock. Nancy watched as everyone stiffened. Frank's hand darted to the speaker button. "Hello!" he called out.

"Your friends are with us," a gravelly, sinister voice replied.

"Who are you?" Ned demanded.

The question was ignored. "You are not to do a thing. That means no more investigations, and no notification of *anyone*—especially the police. And if anything goes wrong—and I mean *anything*—both of our hostages will die."

"Wait a second—"

Frank's protest was cut off by the click of the phone. They all sat dumbfounded as the dial tone droned through the room.

Frank shut off the speaker button. "They're alive. We have a chance."

"That didn't sound like Quinones," Nancy said. She turned to Joe. "Did you get a look at the kidnappers?"

"I couldn't tell much," Joe said. "Their faces were covered, and they were dressed in your basic kidnapper black. The taller one was pretty strong, and the other was kind of skinny, but quick."

Nancy shook her head. "Neither of those descriptions fits Quinones, either."

"They could be a couple of his flunkies," Frank said.

"But what is this guy after?" Ned asked. "First he tries to kill Buck, but now he's holding him hostage with Mercedes. Why?"

"Maybe to get us all," Nancy said. Her comment was greeted with chilly silence as everyone thought.

The shrill ringing of the phone broke the silence. Frank reached over to hit the speaker button again. "Hello!"

"Sergeant Claiborne here. Just checking on your missing-person report. Has the girl shown up yet?"

Nancy looked at Frank. So did Ned and Joe. No one knew what to say.

"Hello? Anybody there?" came Sergeant Claiborne's voice.

Frank leaned toward the phone. "Yes, Sergeant, I'm here. Uh, Mercedes is fine. She was— camping with a friend up in North Padre. Sorry we forgot to call you."

"That's all right. That's why we're checking. Just as long as she's okay."

"Thank you, Sergeant. Good night."

Frank shut off the phone. His face was taut. "If

the police find out, Buck and Mercedes might be killed. It's up to us now. Us and Quinones."

"But what can we do, Frank?" Ned asked, rubbing his bleary eyes. "Go back to his place and wait till the morning?"

"Ned's right," Nancy said. "None of us is going to be of any use if we're completely exhausted."

Frank fought back a yawn. He looked down at his watch. "Sleep well, you guys. I have a feeling we haven't seen anything yet."

Chapter

Seventeen

JOE WAS MISERABLE. In addition to his guilt, his stomach was growling, his head was pounding, his bloodshot eyes were stinging, and his body was aching in places he didn't know existed. And what was worse, he and Frank were stuck spending the morning on the roof of Mercedes's condo.

"I see Ned and Nancy," Frank said, looking through a pair of binoculars. "They're near Quinones's shop. . . . Now they're looking up here. . . . Wave to them!"

Joe threw his arm halfheartedly in the air. Did that hurt!

"Good, they see us," Frank remarked. "Now they're going into the coffee shop across the street from Abe's. That's perfect; they'll see Abe as soon as he goes in." He took the binoculars away from his face and handed them to Joe.

Joe put the lenses up to his eyes. The sight of Abe's Bait and Tackle Shop made him squirm. He could see the alleyways on either side, the refuse-strewn backyard, the dock. . . .

Suddenly he stopped scanning. Putting up to the dock in a small motorboat was a thin, grizzled man with a worn fishing cap. He matched Frank's description of Quinones exactly. "What do you know? There's our man, ready to bait and tackle."

Joe was pleased at his joke, but his brother didn't notice. "Great," Frank said, reaching for the binoculars. "Finally we can do something."

Joe pulled his hands away from Frank's grip. "No way, you had these long enough!"

Frank protested good-naturedly as Joe trained the lenses on the shop. He propped his elbows against the chest-high roof ledge and waited.

And waited . . . and waited . . .

This is ridiculous, Joe thought. It felt as if he were staring at a still photograph. He let the binoculars wander north, out onto the beach. Students were just starting to arrive, setting up blankets, peeling down to their bathing suits. . . .

Joe's eyes lit up. *This* was a view! He could feel his headache disappearing. A group of girls was jogging along the water. Another group was settling in for a morning tan; another was over by the road, buying something at a van marked Ed's Odds and Ends.

"Ed's Odds and Ends," Joe repeated. Why did that sound familiar? "Ed's—"

He nearly dropped the binoculars off the roof. "Frank!" he blurted out. "I think I've got Ed Dougherty!"

This time he did let Frank have the binoculars, and immediately he ran for the stairs. "Hey!" Frank called out. "What about Ned and Nancy?"

But Joe was already inside. As he raced down the stairwell he could hear Frank clattering behind him.

The van was a short run down the beach. As they approached Joe could feel his adrenaline pumping. All he could think about was Iola. Her keys were undoubtedly gone, but it would give him great pleasure to corner their thief—and an attempted murderer!

Joe felt Frank gripping his arm. His brother obviously knew what was going on in his mind. "Stay loose," Frank said. "The guy may be innocent."

"Right—loose." Joe nonchalantly walked up to the van. The side doors were wide open, revealing jewelry display cases and crates full of knickknacks.

Ed Dougherty was an apple-cheeked man with thinning brown hair that was carefully combed across a wide bald spot on his head. Joe noticed he kept his head tilted to one side, probably to keep the hair from falling away and revealing his scalp.

Already Joe didn't like him.

"'Morning," Joe said as nonchalantly as he could. "Looks like you have a lot of interesting stuff."

"Sure do," Dougherty said, standing outside the van. He indicated his collection with a proud sweep of the hand. "Antique jewelry, Indian artifacts, remnants from pirate ships—"

Joe ran his fingers through a bin of unusual seashells. "You specialize in shells, huh?"

"I collect them all myself—right here on Padre Island!"

"But you're missing a shell, aren't you?" Joe's teeth were clenched now. "An *artillery shell?*"

"Joe . . ." Frank admonished.

Dougherty's smile wavered. He looked from Frank to Joe uncertainly. "I—uh—don't under-stand—"

Joe cut him off. "No? Then maybe I can refresh

your memory." Dougherty backed away as Joe took a step closer. "Maybe you remember being a mile or so north of the hotels, back in the tall dunes two afternoons ago."

"I—I couldn't have been there," Dougherty said. "I did work the hotel area that morning, but then I spent the afternoon in Port Isabel."

"Or maybe you can tell us about the goods you managed to steal from Buck Buchanan's condo in South Padre five days ago."

"That would've been my day up on the *north* end. Besides, I don't know anybody named Buchanan." Dougherty's bewildered look was quickly turning into one of anger. "Listen, you, I don't know what you're implying, but I don't like it!"

"Come on, Joe." Frank tried to pull his brother away.

But Joe held back. His eyes had caught something familiar in one of Dougherty's junk bins.

A small set of car keys, fused together.

Iola's keys.

Joe snatched them up. "Where did you get these?"

Dougherty rolled his eyes. "A kid—he found them on the beach and traded them to me for some shells—"

But Joe wasn't hearing a word. Before

Dougherty could finish his sentence, he lunged and was on top of him.

Nancy took the last bite of her corn muffin. She was glad there was a coffee shop across the street from Abe's Bait and Tackle. Especially since she hadn't eaten anything in nearly a day.

"You know, they're going to kick us out of here if we stay too long," Ned said.

Nancy looked at her watch. It was an hour since they had left Frank and Joe on the roof of Mercedes's condo. "Maybe we should take a look at the lunch menu. . . ."

Nancy was about to signal for the waitress when she stopped. Out of the corner of her eye she spotted someone walking toward the bait shop. Someone familiar.

"Rupert Cranston," she said, pointing. "He's the guy whose family has had the feud with the Buchanans."

"You think he's in on this?"

Abe Quinones opened the front door for Rupert. Looking left and right up the street, he backed into the shop, shut the door, and put a Closed sign in the window.

"There's our answer," Nancy said.

They bolted out of their seats, dropped two dollars on the table, and left the coffee shop.

Nancy put on a painter's hat and a pair of sunglasses from her shoulder bag. She tucked her hair into the hat. It wasn't much of a disguise, but it would have to do.

Together they walked across the street. Nancy kept a close eye on the shop window, but it looked deserted inside.

"Now what?" Ned asked.

"I don't know. Look for any signs of movement—"

There was a sudden, dull thud, as if a door had been closed.

"That was from the back of the shop," Nancy said. "Come on!"

She and Ned scrambled around the alley on the left side of the building. They stopped just before the yard and crouched in a shadow, watching.

Quinones wore a gleeful grin that created a cobweb pattern of wrinkles all over his face. He let out a low chuckle and looked admiringly at Rupert. "Good work, my boy. You're a genius!"

Together they scampered over to Quinones's motorboat. "Don't say that until the money starts coming in," Rupert remarked.

"Okay—now!" Nancy whispered.

"Are you kidding?" Ned whispered back. "What if these guys are armed?"

"Frank and Joe have been watching us! They're probably just up the street! Now come on—we can't let them get away."

With that, they burst out of the alley and into the yard. "Hold it!" Nancy yelled. "You're not going anywhere!"

Quinones spun around.

"Is that—Nancy Drew?" Rupert asked.

Quinones's expression hardened to an icy glare. "Friends of Buck, are you?" he snarled.

"Yes, they are!" Rupert said frantically.

"I remember the girl," Quinones said with an evil grin. He slowly stepped toward her, reaching into his back pocket.

Nancy and Ned stopped in their tracks. "Careful," Nancy whispered.

"I don't like spies," Quinones said. "Do you, Rupert?"

"What?" Ned replied.

Come on, Frank and Joe! Nancy thought. Where are you?

"Let me tell you something, kids," Quinones said. "Your friends the Buchanans aren't going to cheat me out of *this* fortune."

When his hand came out of his back pocket, it held a sharp, gleaming bait knife!

161

Chapter

Eighteen

Mr. Quinones, no!" Rupert called out. He hung back by the dock, frightened. "You'll get in trouble!"

"He has a point there," Ned said, backing away.

Quinones let out a guttural chuckle. "So do I. The point of a knife—like the knife that Cord Buchanan stuck in me thirty years ago. The knife that twists inside me deeper and deeper every month—"

Nancy and Ned stopped abruptly. There was a chain-link fence against their backs. Quinones was bearing down on them, so close now that Nancy could smell the alcohol on his breath.

"You know," Quinones said, "bloodsucking

worms are easy to deal with—you just cut 'em up and put 'em on a hook. You bring that message to your boss Buchanan!"

With that, he jumped toward Nancy with the knife.

Nancy ducked away, and the knife cut uselessly into the metal fence. As she fell to the ground Ned grabbed Quinones's arm.

But Quinones yanked his arm back and threw Ned off balance. The two of them tumbled to the ground.

Rupert jumped on top of them, struggling for the knife. Nancy sprang to her feet.

"Arrrrgh!" It was Quinones who emerged from the pile, clutching the knife. He took a wild swing at Ned, ripping part of his shirt sleeve.

Ned scrambled to a standing position right in front of Nancy. He planted his feet and faced Quinones. Rupert raced beside Quinones and pleaded with him: "You're not yourself, Mr. Quinones! Please, let's go!" And Rupert turned and fled.

As Quinones briefly watched him go, Nancy whispered into Ned's ear, "Get his attention and keep it."

Ned feinted a swipe at Quinones's knife. As Quinones reacted Nancy sneaked around to the back wall of the shop.

There, several thick trash bags were propped up, each tied tightly with a string and labeled with an index card. Next to them was a small trowel.

Nancy turned over one of the index cards. It said "Night Crawlers."

Perfect, she thought. Gross, but perfect.

She took the trowel in one hand. Then she pulled the bag open and dug in.

There was a squishy sound as the trowel made contact with the bait. It wasn't going to be pretty.

"Mr. Quinones!" she called out sweetly.

Before Quinones could turn around, he was hit square in the face with a clump of fresh earthworms.

He reacted as Nancy had planned and dropped the knife. He stumbled backward to the edge of the dock. Below him, the water was lapping lazily against the wood pilings.

Thinking fast, Ned did the first thing that came into his mind.

He gave Quinones a push.

Ed Dougherty jumped into his van and tried to pull the door shut. But he wasn't fast enough for Joe. With catlike reflexes, Joe sprang after him, pinning him against the van's back door. Seashells and trinkets spilled out all over the van and Dougherty's few customers backed away in shock.

"Help! He's a maniac!" Dougherty screamed as Joe's hands clutched at his neck.

Frank dived in after his brother. "What are you doing, Joe? Back off!" He grabbed his brother by the collar and yanked.

Joe's jaw was rigid with rage. "He's trying to make fools of us, Frank. He wants to sell Iola's keys as some sort of—of cheap curiosity."

"You want the keys, take the keys!" Dougherty said. "Just get out of here!"

"Come on," Frank said. He pulled Joe out of the van and led him away.

Dougherty spat on his fingers and smoothed down the strands of hair covering his bald spot. When Frank and Joe were safely away, he hopped out. "I'm going to press charges!" he shouted after them, his face a beefy shade of red.

Joe stepped forward, causing Dougherty to flinch. But Frank tightened his grip on Joe's arm and muttered, "Zip it!"

Stepping toward Dougherty, Frank gave him a sincere, apologetic look. "I'm really sorry. You see, my brother's been a little irrational these days. . . ." He knelt down and helped Dougherty pick up the spilled merchandise.

Joe tried to suppress his anger as Frank explained the significance of the keys to Dougherty. Joe walked away, not wanting to hear his personal life laid open to some total creep.

Dougherty's expression began to soften. He nodded sympathetically as Frank finished his story, then walked toward Joe. "Hey, listen," he said. "I didn't know. . . ."

Joe spun around. He felt rage starting to well up again.

"I'm really sorry about your girlfriend," Dougherty continued. "It was a terrible way to go—"

Joe stared at him, dumbfounded. But before he could say a word, Frank took him by the arm again and whisked him away. "No problem, Ed," Frank said over his shoulder. "See you around."

They quickly put distance between themselves and the van.

"How could you let him go?" Joe said. "After what he's done—"

"He's done nothing! Didn't you see the look on his face when you mentioned Buck's name? He had no idea who you were talking about!"

"But the bomb and the keys—"

"Look, Joe. If our lead doesn't work out with Quinones, we'll look into Dougherty again. I just don't think he's involved. Now, let's get out of here. We left Nancy and Ned stranded."

Nancy and Ned! Joe had completely forgotten about them. He and Frank began sprinting down the road toward the center of town.

They reached the coffee shop and found it empty, so they went to Abe's Bait and Tackle. Joe led his brother around the left side of the building to the yard.

And there, sitting beside the gaunt, soggy figure of Abe Quinones, were Ned and Nancy.

"It's about time!" Nancy said, raising an impish eyebrow. "What happened, you hit a lot of traffic?"

Rupert had run up against the fence and was now a willing prisoner of Nancy and Ned's. When he saw Frank and Joe, he shot them a fearful glance.

"I get the feeling something important happened here," Joe said.

Quinones eyed the Hardys warily. "Are these two more of your spies?"

"Mr. Quinones, whatever you're trying is not working," Nancy said. "Now, I suggest you tell us where Buck and Mercedes are. We outnumber you now, and your knife is somewhere at the bottom of the channel—"

"What happened to Mercedes?" Rupert asked, concerned.

"Don't listen to them!" Quinones demanded.

"They sense your weakness—they know you like the girl. They'll stop at nothing to get the secret of our Ultralure."

"Ultra *what?*" Ned asked.

Joe put his hands in the air. "Hold everything! We are definitely not speaking one another's language. First of all, what is all this spy business —and what the heck is Ultralure?"

"First I demand to know where Mercedes is!" Rupert said.

"You were the ones who kidnapped her!" Joe retorted.

"I don't know what you're talking about!"

"That makes six of us!"

There was a long, confused silence. The first to break it was Ned. "You really don't know where she is, do you?"

Rupert shook his head no. "And you really don't know about Ultralure."

"All we want to do is find our friends," Frank said. "There have been some strange things happening on this island—including several attempts on Buck's life. And now this bizarre kidnapping."

"We thought you two were involved," Nancy added, "since both your dad and Mr. Quinones had a feud with Cord Buchanan."

Rupert smirked. "Well, we wouldn't resort to

brute force." He looked at Quinones. "At least *I* wouldn't. That was the whole point—to strike it rich with our brains, not with manipulation like Buchanan. Ultralure will revolutionize the sport of fishing—it uses ultrasound to lure fish. Instead of having to buy different kinds of bait, you just turn a dial to the correct setting."

"And when we put these on the market," Quinones said, "we'll make the Buchanan fortune look like pocket change."

"I'm not so sure I buy this," Joe said. "The kidnappers used your dock as a base of operations."

"I *thought* someone was back here," Quinones said. "One of my nets was missing. Rupert and I were in my basement all night, testing our product."

"You see," Rupert explained, "we had isolated a certain frequency that acted on a specific type of marine life that I had been collecting—"

"Don't tell me," Ned said. "Portuguese men-of-war."

"Exactly," Rupert answered, giving Nancy a quizzical look. "But a few days ago I came home to find that someone had broken in and stolen the whole tankful. We figured Buchanan was sabotaging our experiment."

"So we've been doing our experiments at my

place," Quinones added. "Only now we're working twice as fast, so we can finish before Buchanan strikes again. I even closed up shop at night. Busiest time of the week."

Nancy nodded. It was all falling into place. When she looked at Frank and Joe, their eyes were saying the same thing.

They'd been following the wrong lead all along. Quinones had been framed.

Chapter

Nineteen

So THE QUESTION IS, who was it that called Buck and Joe last night?" Ned said.

"Someone who knew that Mr. Quinones had a grudge against Buck's dad," Frank replied. "The plan must have been to lure Nancy into Abe's Bait and Tackle and plant clues to make her think Mr. Quinones was involved."

"Only Joe got there instead of me, and too early," Nancy added. "The kidnappers hadn't even broken in yet."

"The worst part about it," Frank said, "is that the kidnappers have exactly whom they want— and we don't know what they plan to do with him."

Joe shook his head with frustration. "Now

what? Six days on Padre Island, we've got robberies and attempted murders leading us nowhere—and I don't even have a suntan!"

"I have an idea," Nancy said suddenly. "Follow me!"

Leaving Rupert and Quinones behind, she led Frank, Joe, and Ned back out to the street. Together they ran the few blocks to a familiar spot on the pier—Roy's Aquatic World.

Roy peeked over the top of his newspaper when they came in. "Can't keep away from the buried treasure, eh?"

"You bet," Nancy answered playfully. "We just want enough to pay for our plane fare."

He chuckled and opened a notebook on his desk. "Let me just get your sizes again. . . ."

As Roy looked through the book Ned whispered to Nancy, "What are we doing here?"

"We're going back to the beginning," Nancy replied. "To that wreck we saw our first day here. I have a feeling Buck saw something there he wasn't supposed to see."

"But we searched the whole thing so carefully," Frank said.

"Nancy's right," Joe protested. "We've got to look closer."

Nancy smiled. She could see visions of treasure chests dancing in Joe's head.

They grabbed the suits that Roy had draped over the counter and disappeared into the changing rooms. Minutes later they ran back through the shop, took the keys from the counter, and headed out the front door. Roy watched as they climbed into their launch. As they started up he waved to them and shouted, "Good luck!"

Ned quickly navigated out to the wreck site and dropped anchor. The sky was crystal clear, perfect for visibility.

Nancy reached for her mask. "Let's go," she said.

Leading the way, she flipped in. This time it was easy to find the coral wall. Just beyond it, the wreck loomed into sight.

The broken porthole was still there, as was the lopsided mast—everything untouched.

Or so she thought. As she swam around to look for the opening in the hull her eyes opened wide.

It had been welded shut.

Nancy propelled herself closer. A large metal sheet now covered the opening. Small fish could swim in and out of the gaps between the spot welding, but nothing larger.

The three boys swam next to Nancy and examined the metal barrier. Ned reached his fingers under one of the gaps. He pulled hard, and one of the spot-welds did give way.

He pulled again. With a muffled popping noise, another weld broke.

Now the gap was about six inches wide. Nancy felt a rush of hope. These guys were better kidnappers than welders, she thought. The four of them yanked as hard as they could.

But the sheet wouldn't budge. Finally Joe pulled away and banged on it.

Just then Ned held up his index finger. When the other three looked at him, he began a crude pantomime, his hands gripping an imaginary handle, pushing down.

A crowbar, Nancy realized. She remembered seeing one on the deck of the launch on which they had just come out. Ned pointed upward; obviously he remembered it, too. Nancy nodded enthusiastically, and Ned immediately started swimming toward the surface.

It looked as though Frank and Joe had caught on, too. They gave Ned the thumbs-up sign and swam around the wreck, inspecting it for clues.

Nancy thrust forward to join them. After a few minutes, she heard a strange, high-pitched thrumming noise above them. It started softly and then quickly grew louder and louder.

Nancy looked up. She knew she'd heard that sound before, and it took her only a moment to identify it.

It had to be a cigarette boat!

With a strong kick, she shot up through the water. No cigarette boat would ever come out this far, unless—

In the distance there was a flash of light above the surface of the water. Nancy reeled backward from the vibration of an immense shock wave.

Terror swept through her. The blast had gone off right where their launch was.

Ned—he was there!

Chapter

Twenty

An INVOLUNTARY SCREAM ripped up through Nancy. Her mouth opened and the mouthpiece dropped out. She started to say "Ned," but in the murky depths of the Gulf, there was only silence.

She launched herself up even as planks of wood began to descend. But she hadn't gotten very far when she was rocked by another explosion—one closer, louder.

It wasn't only debris that was falling from the surface. Nancy also identified dark, heavy metallic objects as they plunged past her. Each one was farther from the launch—and closer to the wreck and her.

She was already too numb to be shocked when one of them exploded practically in front of her.

She was forced back toward the wreck. Now there was another explosion just above her.

But none of it mattered. Not when Ned needed her.

She started to kick back up, but a firm grip stopped her. She turned around. It was Frank. He mouthed, "You're coming with me, like it or not!"

The next explosion was so close it rattled Nancy's jaw. Frank pulled her toward a coral formation far from the wreck. Joe was waiting behind it, and the three of them held on to the jagged rock, sheltered from the blasts.

They peered out cautiously. The welded side of the ship was completely visible. Three explosives dropped near it.

Depth charges, Nancy realized. Whoever was dropping them wanted to destroy the ship.

Or, more likely, destroy the people who were daring to intrude. They weren't satisfied with hurting or killing Ned, Nancy thought. They want us, too. She felt tears of rage and sorrow well up.

The first explosion sent shock waves through the water, pushing Nancy, Frank, and Joe backward. The second one went off nearer to them, breaking off part of their coral wall.

Nancy braced herself for the third.

This was a different noise, sharper than the first two. It was followed by the thrum of the boat, which faded quickly into the distance. The three waited for a few seconds, then swam to the wall and looked over.

Dark clouds of sand and seaweed, shaken up by the blasts, billowed in front of them. It was impossible to see the wreck—or what was left of it.

But Nancy didn't care about it. It was Ned. He was gone—just like that. It didn't seem possible. How could they have done that to him? And worse, why had she let him go alone to the surface? Feelings of anger, shock, guilt, and grief all crashed together in her mind until they canceled one another out, and Nancy was left numb. She stared as shadows passed through the muck —fish, clumps of refuse, driftwood. . . .

Something large and mobile caught Nancy's attention—a long shadow, definitely something alive. Her eyes followed it as it glided from side to side. She was suddenly tense. What was it she had read about sharks being attracted to distant vibrations? Were there sharks in the Gulf of Mexico?

She didn't want to find out. Grabbing Frank's and Joe's arms, she began to swim away.

But the Hardy brothers pulled her back. Frank shook his head and pointed over the wall.

Nancy took another look. The swimming silhouette was closer to them now. Frank was right—it wasn't a shark. It had arms and legs, and a scuba suit.

They sent someone down to see if we're alive, Nancy said to herself. He's probably got a gun.

This time it was Frank who pulled Nancy back. But he didn't swim away, and Nancy knew why. Like her, he was holding on to the slim hope that the person might be—

Nancy was disbelieving. It *was* Ned! The brown hair was unmistakable, as were his broad shoulders.

With strong thrusts of her legs, Nancy swam toward him. If she hadn't been underwater, she would have screamed with joy.

Ned gave her a thumbs-up sign and wiped his brow as if to say "Whew!" Nancy had no idea how he had escaped, but the explanation would have to wait.

He motioned her and the Hardys to follow him. They made their way through the murky water, until a familiar shadow faced them.

The sunken ship's mast had broken off. Now only a stub protruded. The angle of the ship was different, too—the blast had knocked it far onto its side.

And the metal sheet on the side of the ship had been torn loose. It hung from one spot-weld, revealing the gaping hole it had once covered.

The four of them raced toward the hole. Because of the ship's new angle, the hole faced straight up. Sunlight was beginning to filter in, reflecting off a wall within the ship.

When they'd seen the wall earlier, even in the beam from their flashlights, it had appeared solid and smooth. But now they could see that there was a hidden compartment, which had been wrenched open by the blast. Three small dark plastic bags, tied shut with nylon twine, had spilled out the door and onto the sand.

Joe was the first to get to the bags. He pulled the twine off one and looked inside.

Nancy peered over his shoulder—and her heart skipped a beat. Sharp light rays from gold and silver reflected in her eyes.

Joe had finally found his treasure!

Chapter

Twenty-One

JOE QUICKLY TIED the bag shut and scooped it up while Nancy and Frank picked up the other two.

Joe then looked into the trapdoor, and a grin spread across his face. He pointed with broad gestures inside.

When Nancy peered through, she saw five or six more bags lying against a wall in the secret compartment. She reached in and grabbed one, and the three boys took the rest.

They began to swim upward but didn't get far. Each bag was only about the size of an over-stuffed wallet, but they were heavy.

Nancy knew that they'd have to get rid of some drag. She signaled to get everyone's attention, then reached for the weights that were attached to her belt. Weights were helpful for scuba diving; without them, a diver would have to fight to keep from floating up.

But now the weights were unnecessary. Nancy unhooked hers and let them drop. Then she attached two of the bags to her belt, where the weights had been.

Ned, Frank, and Joe did the same, and together they swam to the surface. Nancy had to pull furiously with her arms because of the bags. When they broke the surface, Joe yanked off his mask and let out a howl of delight. "We did it!"

Nancy threw her arms around Ned. "I thought you were caught in the blast!"

"I lost my way," he replied. "Lucky for me. When the bomb went off, I was nowhere near it!"

"Come on," Joe said. "It's going to be tough getting back with all this weight." He plunged underwater and began swimming toward the beach.

Nancy looked ahead of her. It was at least five miles. "I don't know, guys. This stuff is incredibly heavy."

"Don't even *think* of ditching it," Joe said. "If you can't hack it, give me a bag."

Can't hack it? Who did Joe think he was dealing with? Nancy thought. She gave him a nonchalant smile and said, "No, thanks. I was just afraid it might weigh *you* down."

With that, Nancy put on her mask and began swimming. The first few yards weren't too bad, but then she felt herself sinking with each stroke. The sandy bottom was getting closer. Nancy looked up. Ned, Frank, and Joe were far ahead but also sinking. She imagined herself having to crawl along the bottom all the way to the shore.

If that's the only way to get this stuff to shore, Nancy said to herself, that's what I'm going to have to do.

She checked her oxygen gauge—and knew she was dead wrong. It was almost empty. If she was lucky, she'd last a quarter of the way.

Ahead of her, the boys were struggling to get to the surface. No one wanted to cut any of their bags loose.

They're not looking at their gauges, Nancy realized. She had to get to them and warn them.

She began untying her bags—there was no choice.

Then the distant hum of a boat engine broke the silence.

What incredible timing, she thought. It took a burst of extra energy to get back to the surface—and when she did the boys were already there. To Nancy's left, a boat was cutting through the water toward them, sending up sea spray on either side.

"Over here!" Nancy shouted as loud as she could.

Immediately she wished she hadn't. As the boat came nearer she could see its long, narrow shape.

The shape of a cigarette boat.

Ned, Frank, and Joe looked paralyzed. The boat was heading for the gap between them and Nancy at full throttle.

Nancy frantically reached for her belt again.

But just then the boat's engine cut off. "Hey!" a voice called out.

Nancy looked at the boat. Two bronze-skinned, burly guys were standing up, waving at her. Each had on sunglasses and a white smear of zinc oxide on his nose.

She immediately recognized one of them as the new lifeguard on the beach near Mercedes's condo, the one who had replaced Claire's legendary Bruce. "You all okay?" he asked. "We heard this noise—"

The boat floated past them, then turned around. "We're fine!" Nancy shouted back. "But we're running out of oxygen!"

"Well, come on in," the guy said. "We'll squeeze you all in somehow."

"Who are you guys?" Joe asked.

"Rick Hamlin," the lifeguard responded. "This is my buddy Willie. We just got off work and were taking a spin when we heard some kind of explosion. What happened—your boat blow up or something?"

"Uh, yeah," Frank said quickly. "I don't know how the engine could have caught on fire like that. It's a good thing we were underwater."

"Lucky," Willie replied, shaking his head. "That's the first I ever heard of something like that happening."

Nancy couldn't believe they bought the excuse. Fortunately, Frank changed the subject before they could ask questions. "Did you see another cigarette boat going by in the opposite direction?"

"Yeah," Rick said, putting the boat in gear. "We were going to stop it to find out what had happened, but it was too far away."

As the boat traveled toward the shore Nancy thought of another question. "Aren't you the lifeguard who replaced—what's his name—"

"Bruce Comins? Yep! How did you know?" Rick said with a perplexed smile.

"I saw you over by the condos," Nancy replied. "What ever happened to Bruce, anyway?"

Rick shrugged. "Beats me. Probably got bored

and left. I mean, he didn't really need the money."

"What do you mean?" Frank asked.

"Well, he always hung out in these really expensive clothes, ate out at the best restaurants. He probably lifeguarded just to meet girls. Whatever it was, he just up and disappeared one day." He looked at the shore, which was quickly approaching. "Where do you want to go?"

Nancy could see Roy's to the left, next to the pier. To the right was a small, scrubby stretch of beach between docks. "Let us off on the sand over there," she said. "We have to figure out how we're going to explain this to Roy."

Rick gave her a knowing smile. "Gotcha." He glided to the shore and let them out.

"Good luck," he said as they got off the boat.

Nancy watched as the cigarette boat disappeared down the coast. Then she surveyed the beach around her. Behind it there was a small, abandoned storage building.

"Come on!" Nancy called out. She ran to the building and ducked into the shadow beside one of its walls.

There, the four of them opened the bags and looked inside.

"This is incredible!" Joe exclaimed, letting

gold jewelry spill out of his bag. "We've hit the jackpot!"

"I'm not so sure," Frank said. Inside his bag was a sealed flat plastic pouch. He ripped it open to reveal a stack of papers that looked like large checks. "Bearer bonds," he said. "Payable to whoever signs them."

Ned had ripped open another watertight pouch. "This is crazy," he said. "These are stock certificates."

But Nancy wasn't listening. She was eyeing an item in her own bag—a diamond bracelet that had the initials *CB* stamped on the inside.

"Claire Bouchard," she said softly.

"What?" Joe replied, cocking his head at her.

Nancy put the bracelet down and stared at the stash that now littered the ground. It was all clear now.

"I have news for you, guys," she said. "Something tells me this stuff did *not* belong to Jean Laffite."

Chapter

Twenty-Two

FRANK TOOK THE BRACELET and looked it over. "Bingo."

Ned gave Nancy and Frank a bewildered look. "What are you guys talking about?" he asked.

"This is the bracelet that was taken from Claire's apartment," Frank said. "And these stocks, these bonds—it all fits the description of the stuff stolen from the condos."

Ned shook his head in amazement, looking at their catch. "These guys were really organized, weren't they?"

"They must have been," Nancy replied. "Their timing was incredible. For each of the break-ins, they knew exactly when to show up."

"They had enough time—and knowledge—to

pick through and take only portable valuables," Joe added. "Stuff that could be resold or cashed in."

Frank nodded. "They also knew exactly where to look—Claire's jewelry box, Jennifer's safe—"

"Someone young must have been involved," Nancy said. "Someone who blended in, who was a regular around the condos. He could easily case whatever apartment he was invited into. And he'd have no problem figuring out schedules."

"Well, *I'm* not the detective," Ned said with a shrug, "but I think it was that lifeguard Bruce. I mean, both those girls knew him and trusted him."

Nancy looked at her boyfriend. "You may be right, Ned, but how do we explain his disappearance? If he ran away, wouldn't he have taken the stuff with him?"

"Maybe he didn't run away," Frank interjected. "Maybe he was killed."

Ned looked at him doubtfully.

"The crooks could have had a fight over the division of the loot," Frank added.

"Yeah, but then wouldn't there be a bod—"

Ned didn't finish the sentence. He looked around, his eyes registering a look of grim realization. "I guess that's why they wanted Buck. . . ."

"He *saw* Bruce's body, hidden in the wreck," Nancy said. "Someone must have found out, because by the time we got there, the body was gone!"

"But how did they find out we saw it?" Frank asked. "We didn't tell anybody—or did we?"

Joe's face lit up. "Of course we did! Roy, at the rental shop. He knew we'd found the wreck. We blabbed about it when we went back to look at it."

"Right! Then he told us to look on *land* for the treasure!" Nancy added.

"And he was the only person who knew where we were just now when our launch was bombed!" Ned said.

Joe pounded his fist against the side of the building. "How could I be so stupid? That voice over the telephone at Mercedes's—it was Roy's, trying to sound tough."

"He sure does fit the bill," Frank said. "He's pretty young, he hangs out at the beach—and he must know everybody who lives in South Padre. Or at least the ones who rent boats and scuba equipment."

Ned smiled ironically. "Sounds perfect. He waits till they're on the water, sneaks over to their apartment, robs them—then charges them for his time."

Nancy reviewed the events of the week for a moment. Then she shook her head. "There's something wrong. We talked about the wreck in front of him the day *after* we found it. But the body was already gone by that day. We couldn't have said anything to Roy that first day in the rain because he was out of his office when we got back. And I don't think we talked about it in front of Roy's assistant."

"He was out of his office because he was robbing Buck's apartment," Frank said. "Someone must have tipped him off—but who?"

"Beats me," Joe said. "What's the difference, anyway? Why don't we go after the lead we *do* have?"

Nancy nodded. "Joe's right. I think it's time to go on the offensive." She looked up the street and spotted a pay phone. "Anybody got a quarter?"

Ned, Frank, and Joe returned blank looks. "We could trade in one of these," Joe said straight-faced, holding up a gold necklace.

Nancy laughed. "Come on, let's see what he says to a collect call."

Quickly they scooped up the valuables, put them in the bags, and trotted out to the phone booth.

Nancy picked up the receiver. Down the road she could see Roy's shop—and Roy. He was visible through the side window, talking on the phone. As soon as he put it down, Nancy dialed the operator and placed a collect call.

"Hello?" came Roy's voice. She watched him carefully.

"Collect call from Nancy Drew," the operator droned. "Will you accept?"

There was a momentary silence.

"Nancy Drew?" Roy finally said, with a hushed, disbelieving tone.

"Yes, sir."

"I'll take the call. . . ." Roy sat on a stool with his back to the counter.

"Hello, Roy. Nice day!" Nancy said, with enthusiastic sweetness.

"Yes—yes, it is," Roy answered uncertainly. "Uh, where are you?"

"I have your merchandise," Nancy remarked, ignoring the question.

Another silence.

When Roy spoke up, his voice was a whisper. "My—merchandise?"

"And I don't mean your launch. Your insurance will cover that—if you have a bombing-by-the-owner clause, that is."

"What do you want?" Roy rasped.

Nancy could tell she'd hit home. When he

answered, there wasn't a trace of confusion in his voice. "A trade, Roy. Your stash for my friends. What do you say?"

"All right." He sounded relieved. "Come to my shop tonight at—"

"No. It has to be someplace with lots of people. Someplace where you can't get away with anything funny."

"All right, all right . . ." She watched him get up from his stool and pace behind the counter. "How about the Dos Banditos restaurant tonight? Do you know it?"

"Yes." She put her hand over the receiver and mouthed "Dos Banditos" to Ned, Frank, and Joe.

Frank nodded, then said one word: "Proof."

She took her hand away from the phone. "Fine, under one condition—we want proof that they're alive. In a half hour call me back at this number"—she looked at the white strip below the phone's buttons—"five five five one one five four, and play me a tape of both their voices. They must tell us they're okay *and* today's date and the time."

"What? I don't have time to—"

"There's an awful lot of valuable stuff here, Mr. Manvell, and the police would be—"

"Okay, okay, I'll do it!" With an angry, crashing sound, the phone clicked off.

Nancy hung up. She felt her heart pumping like crazy. "We've got him," she said simply.

Joe's eyes were riveted on the shop. "Look!" he said.

Nancy glanced over to see Roy frantically placing another call. He barked something into the phone, hung up, and disappeared from the window.

"He must be getting in touch with his cohort," Frank said. "We'd better hurry in order to tail him."

"I'll stay here," Nancy said. "Someone has to answer his call or he'll be suspicious."

"I'll stay with you," Ned said.

"No, Ned," Nancy said. "I mean, what if Roy has two or three accomplices? You have to help Frank and Joe try to free our friends. As soon as Roy calls, I'll head over to Dos Banditos. You meet me there."

"Then what?" Joe asked.

Nancy gave him a meaningful look. "That depends on whether or not you have Buck and Mercedes."

At that moment Roy stormed out of his shop and ran toward the dock, clutching a small tape machine.

Nancy, Ned, Frank, and Joe all ducked behind the old building. They heard the roar of a cigarette-boat engine.

"Great," Frank said. "How are we going to follow that?"

Joe grinned. "No problem. Stick with me."

As the cigarette boat pulled away Joe raced toward the pier. Ned and Frank followed him to a long fiberglass powerboat with the name *Banzai* emblazoned on the hull. Joe hopped in and pulled open a hatch on the wooden floor. Inside the hatch there was a collection of tools. He rummaged around and pulled out a set of keys. "We're in business!"

"Wha— How did you know about this?" Ned asked, amazed.

"It belongs to a friend of Buck's," he said, shoving the key in the ignition. "And it's just as fast as any flimsy little cigarette boat. We took it out yesterday when we were looking for Mercedes. He showed me where he hid the spare key."

Ned untied the boat as Joe started the engine. Immediately he maneuvered it away from the pier and zoomed out into the Gulf.

The sun was just setting behind them as they followed Roy, keeping a healthy distance between them. Joe made sure to keep the headlights off and the throttle as low as possible.

Before long they couldn't even see Padre Island. Roy kept speeding away, making no turn back to the shore.

"Where is he keeping them?" Frank asked. "In Europe?"

The answer came sooner than expected. On the horizon was a small desert island, surrounded by inlets and coves. Palm trees swayed in the breeze, their dusky silhouettes looking like giant fans.

Joe cut the engine. He could barely make out the long, thin shape of Roy's boat as it pulled into one of the coves. And the only sign of Roy himself was a speck of white moving from the dock into the grove of trees.

"Look what we found, guys," Joe remarked. "Gilligan's Island."

Joe pulled out a set of oars and quietly guided the boat into another cove, hidden from Roy's pier. The three boys clambered out of the boat and pulled it onto the beach.

A pinprick of amber light flickered in the distance, at the top of a hill. Frank took the lead, stepping around scrub brush, making sure to stay well hidden behind the four- and five-foot sand dunes.

The light grew sharper as they moved closer to it. From its bobbing movement, Joe knew it was a flashlight.

At the sound of muffled voices, the boys stopped. Huddled behind a sand dune, they listened closely.

It was tough to make out words, but "April" and "six forty-five" were clear enough. And one of the voices was definitely Buck's.

A clicking sound echoed dully in the humid air. Then, quickly, the flashlight began the descent toward the cove.

The three boys waited for the rumbling of the cigarette-boat engine, then ran out from behind their dune.

"Buck! Mercedes!" Frank called out.

"Frank?" came an incredulous voice. Joe could see a rustling on top of the hill, then the shadows of two figures rising to their feet.

"Hey, look at this, Mercedes!" Buck cried out. "The cavalry has come to our rescue!"

They scampered down the hill. Mercedes threw her arms around Frank and Ned, laughing with relief. Buck locked his arm around Joe's shoulder.

"How the heck did you do this?" Buck asked. "Ol' Roy just made us record some kind of tape."

"We'll tell you all about it on the way back," Joe said. "Let's get out of here!"

. . . and it's six forty-five in the evening, with a lovely sunset. Wish you could join us—

The tape clicked off, and Nancy heard Roy's voice say, "There's your proof. Now I want to collect on my end of this deal."

"Fine," Nancy replied. "Just bring them to Dos Banditos one hour from now. Just you and them—nobody else. I'll meet you there."

Nancy hung up the phone. It had taken Roy more than half an hour to get back to her, and she had begun to fret. But the voices were unquestionably Buck's and Mercedes's, and the dates and times checked out.

There wasn't any time to lose. Nancy scooped up all the bags and staggered to the road. It was only then that she realized how ridiculous she looked—barefoot, wearing a wet suit, and clutching an armload of plastic bags.

She finally made it to Mercedes's condo, peeled off her wet suit, and changed into jeans and a blouse. Then she bolted for the door.

At the last moment before leaving, she

stopped. The bags! She had left them out on the couch.

She turned back into the room. It dawned on her that she hadn't thought about what to do with them. Should she give Roy the stolen goods? Obviously it wasn't the *right* thing to do, but what about the lives of her friends? Was it worth putting them in jeopardy?

But what if she lived up to her end of the deal? The crime would be back to where it started—a man probably killed and thousands of dollars' worth of jewelry stolen.

Besides, there was no way Roy would show up at Dos Banditos without some trick up his sleeve.

Nancy made up her mind. She ran upstairs and stuffed the bags between the mattress and box spring.

The run to Dos Banditos was long and tiring. By the time she got there, perspiration had soaked her blouse. She walked up to the door, where a group of four guys were bellowing with laughter.

"Hey," one of them said when he saw Nancy, "you look like you could use one of these!" He ripped off a can of soda from a six-pack and tossed it to her.

His throw was wide. The can flipped end over

end through the air to the left of Nancy. "Thanks. But I hope your coach didn't see that," she said, picking it up.

"Who-o-o-oa!" one of them said, slapping the passer on the back. "The coach has spies everywhere."

Just as Nancy was about to open the can, she heard a familiar voice. "Where have you *been?* Did you find Mercedes?"

"Bess!" Nancy said, spinning around. "Later, I'll tell you later, okay?" she said.

Bess approached her with a radiant smile. Her hair was pulled back on both sides with a pair of brightly colored lacquer combs, and she wore a frilly white Mexican dress with a gold coin hung on a gold chain around her neck. Behind her was George, dressed in a short skirt and tank top.

Nancy wanted to spill all the details of the case to her friends, but not in public.

"Guess who's been shopping?" George said with a wry smile, pointedly looking at Bess.

"Do you like the outfit?" Bess asked, spinning around. "I picked it up at an incredible crafts fair that we happened to find while we were searching for Mercedes. And look at this necklace—it's just like the one Taryn wears. The gold coin is a replica of an old Mexican coin. Isn't it fantastic?"

"Beautiful," Nancy said. But Bess's wardrobe was the last thing on her mind. She cast a glance over her shoulder into the restaurant. "Listen, I have a lot to tell you. Why don't we go inside?"

"Good idea," George said. "Just tell us one thing—is Mercedes all right?" Nancy nodded and smiled.

When Nancy turned back, Bess had been drawn into a conversation with the group of guys. Coyly fingering her gold necklace, she laughed at someone's joke just then.

There was something familiar about that necklace, something besides the fact that Nancy had seen one like it on Taryn. . . .

George interrupted her thoughts. "I guess it's just you and me."

"Yep." Nancy put the can of soda in her shoulder bag as she and George walked into the restaurant. She scanned the room, but there was no sign of Roy. Her attention was caught by a series of framed softball-team photos on a nearby wall. Each one was dated, year by year, in descending order. Nancy could pick out Taryn's face in every one of them. In fact, there was a shot of only Taryn, looking much younger, dated four years ago. She was in uniform on a pitcher's mound, her eyes focused on home plate.

Underneath it were the words "Padre Island

Championship Game—Winning Pitcher, Taryn Quinones.

Quinn . . . Quinones. Taryn must have changed her name, Nancy realized. A statement of Abe Quinones's flashed through her mind. "We was never rich, but my daughter's doin' okay. . . ."

Taryn was Abe's daughter. It seemed hard to believe she was related to that bitter old man.

And that's when it all hit her. The Quinones-Buchanan feud . . . replicas of old Mexican coins . . . Taryn's necklace . . .

She stopped cold. "How could I have missed it?" she asked out loud.

"What? What's wrong?" George asked.

"The old coin we found in the wreck. It came from Taryn's necklace. *She's* the other accomplice!"

Chapter

Twenty-Three

G EORGE LOOKED BAFFLED. "Taryn? The waitress? Are you serious?"

"Yes." Nancy pulled her aside, to a secluded area. She lowered her voice to an excited hush. "Think of it, George. Taryn hasn't worn that necklace since the day we got here—"

"Maybe it was stolen," George suggested.

"If it was, don't you think she would have mentioned something about it when we were discussing the robberies? No, she must have lost it while diving."

"But—diving with a necklace? Who would do that?"

"Someone in a hurry to get rid of a body, that's

who. Someone who heard us talking about that body over dinner and was afraid we'd go back out and find it." Suddenly images flashed into her mind—clues that had eluded her until then. "It all makes sense. *Taryn* was the one who told us where to look for Ed Dougherty, and sent us to a place where we almost got blown up!

"And that explains the strained look on her face when she saw us after the explosion—she couldn't believe we were still alive. Then she stuck around while Frank was figuring out strategies. No wonder she started hanging out with Frank."

"It sort of makes sense," George said, "but *why* would she do it, Nancy? This is pretty heavy stuff to be involved in!"

Nancy pointed to the softball photo. "Her real name is Quinones. The kidnappers were hiding Mercedes at Abe Quinones's Bait and Tackle Shop. Now, who else besides Abe would have access to his shop? His daughter would!"

"Or Abe himself," George said. "He's the one who's angry at Buck's dad—"

Nancy shook her head. "No, we're pretty sure he's not involved. He's got his own method of getting even with Cord Buchanan—some bizarre invention. But *Taryn* could hold a fierce grudge. I mean, imagine spending your whole life listening

to your father complain about a lost fortune—
that has to affect you!"

"I guess she's taking back from Padre Island
the money her dad let slip away, huh?"

"Something like that—"

"Sssh!" Nancy warned. Over George's shoulder, she spotted Taryn walking toward them with
a grin across her face. Her hands were folded in
front of her, casually holding a small, empty
cocktail tray. "Hey there, what're y'all doing?"
she said.

"Waiting for the guys," Nancy said, trying to
sound nonchalant. She rolled her eyes and
smiled. "They're late, as usual."

"No, they're not," Taryn said cheerfully.
"They're waiting out back. They told me they
wanted to talk to you out there."

Nancy's mind was racing. Was this a trick?
Why wouldn't they come inside? Would they ask
Taryn to get Nancy? Did they suspect her?

And what about Roy? That other phone call he
had made at his shop must have been to Taryn—
he must have tipped her off. Was *he* waiting
outside, without Buck and Mercedes?

She looked into Taryn's eyes, which had become cold and steely gray. Then she looked
down—and saw the glint of *real* steel under
Taryn's tray.

It was the barrel of a small pistol.

"Uh, I think we ought to go, George," Nancy said.

George swallowed. "Yeah," she said.

Nancy frantically searched her mind for some way to disarm Taryn.

As if reading her mind, Taryn said, "Roy has his eye on you through the side window. He has a gun, too, and he also has your boyfriend. You try *anything,* and Roy's liable to do something rash."

Nancy looked out the window, but it was too dark to see anything. Maybe Taryn was bluffing, but it wasn't worth the chance. Not in a crowded restaurant. Nancy and George followed her into the kitchen.

Taryn led them outside through a side door. To their right Bess was still standing with the guys. To their left was the back corner of the restaurant, where Roy was all alone. A weak outdoor exit light shone down on his face, distorting it into an evil mask.

"Where are the others?" Nancy asked.

"Beats me," Roy said. "Why don't we go find them?"

"Move," Taryn ordered, her hands still gripping the gun.

Nancy and George walked up to Roy. Taryn

dropped the cocktail tray to uncover her gun, and Roy pulled out a semiautomatic pistol.

Taryn and Roy hustled the girls through the alley, into a side street, and out onto a dock, where Roy's boat was waiting.

"Wh-where are you taking us?" George stammered as Roy forced her and Nancy onto the boat.

"Oh, Taryn and I have discussed a great ceremony for you," he replied. He untied the mooring rope, then quickly started up the engine. "It's a variation on an honor bestowed to war heroes at sea. Only we think it should also apply to despicable underage spies."

He chuckled. Nancy hated these melodramatic word games. "What ceremony, Roy?" she asked matter-of-factly.

When Roy turned to answer, his face had hardened. "It's called 'burial at sea.'"

Chapter

Twenty-Four

"So Freddy rises to the challenge and downs three chicken-fried steaks in one sitting—with hot sauce! You should have seen his face, man!"

The four guys around Bess roared with laughter. But Bess wasn't listening. She was too worried.

It *had* to be a gun, she thought. It looked like one.

No, she said to herself. I've been spending too much time around detectives. Why would *Taryn* have a gun?

She ran through the scene in her mind. The flash of metal, the way Taryn turned her back as soon as she got out of the restaurant, the awkward way she held her tray . . .

Nancy and George didn't look too thrilled either. But it could be that they were all having some sort of important meeting about the case.

A voice inside told her she should get involved. But that was the voice that always seemed to get her into trouble. What would Nancy do in this situation? she tried to decide.

She turned back to the boys, who were now acting out a football story that they all found unbelievably funny.

The choice was clear. Ducking away, she hurried toward the back of the building.

"Nancy?" she called into the dark alleyway. "George?"

No answer. But from a nearby pier, she heard the thrum of a boat engine starting up. She ran the few steps to get a good look.

Gliding out into the Gulf, illuminated only by the pale yellow dock lights, was a white cigarette boat. She couldn't see much, but there were definitely four people aboard. And one of them had long red hair.

Nancy was in trouble—big trouble. Bess knew she had to call the police. She could barely feel her feet beneath her as she ran back to Dos Banditos.

She barreled through the front entrance.

"Bess!" someone shouted.

Bess didn't turn around. She flew down the stairs toward the rest rooms, where the pay phones were.

There was a clatter of footsteps behind her.

"What happened? Where's Nancy?" The voice was Ned's. Bess picked up the receiver and dialed 911. Glancing over her shoulder, she saw that Frank, Joe, Buck, and Mercedes were with Ned. The boys were wearing wet suits and no shoes.

"She and George have been kidnapped," Bess said breathlessly. "By Roy and Taryn. They brought her to the pier around back and took her out on a cigarette—"

Before she could finish, Frank, Joe, and Ned were taking the stairs two at a time. Buck followed, but Frank stopped him. "Stay here with Mercedes and Bess," he called back.

As Bess gave the police a report she noticed that Mercedes and Buck were holding hands.

"Can you untie our hands now?" Nancy asked. "I don't think we're much danger to you all the way out here."

Taryn looked at Roy, who was steering the boat with one arm while training a semiautomatic pistol on Nancy with the other. He glanced back at the shore, now a receding string of tiny lights.

After thinking a moment, he nodded. Taryn untied them.

Nancy and George shook their arms out, keeping their eyes on Taryn.

"You know, you guys made a big mistake," she said, her voice thick with anger. "You agreed to bring the goods along."

"*If* you brought Buck and Mercedes," Nancy answered coolly. "I didn't see them."

"Oh, you think you're smart, don't you?" Roy shouted to be heard over the engine noise. "You think we won't do anything to you because you know where the stuff is. Well, let me tell you something—we have other ways of finding out. Better ways. Like using your strange, *permanent* disappearance to set an example for your pals. I've killed once, and it was easy for me."

Nancy felt George shivering beside her. It was contagious; Nancy fought to keep herself still.

Keeping the gun trained on her captives, Taryn rummaged through Nancy's shoulder bag for the third time. With an exclamation of disgust, she dropped it on the floor.

The can of soda rolled out, and Nancy watched it settle against her foot, dented from its fall on the grass earlier.

Taryn rubbed her forehead. Her features were

211

pinched, nervous. "Where's that island, Roy?" she asked.

"What island?" he answered with a chuckle. "Not this time, sweetheart. The stakes are a little different."

Taryn blanched. "You mean we really are . . ."

She let her voice drift off. Nancy felt a shudder. The "burial at sea" had been a bluff to Taryn.

But not to Roy.

"Nancy . . ." George's voice was a soft, desperate moan as the boat pitched on a sudden choppy area.

"I want to get us past this rough patch," Roy shouted. "Then we'll let 'em have it."

"Right," Taryn said, with less conviction than before.

Just then, a few distant, rhythmic splashes of white caught Nancy's eye off to her left and behind Taryn. Something was cutting through the water toward them. She couldn't hear it; the cigarette-boat engine was too loud. But it *had* to be another boat.

The boat pitched again, and the can of soda rolled away and up against Nancy's foot again. The can of soda that had been thrown, dropped, bounced around, and dropped again . . .

Nancy felt a surge of hope. She remembered something she had once used in a situation similar to this. Suddenly she started shaking—she let herself shake. Taryn looked at her, panicked. Good, Nancy thought. She thinks I've cracked.

"P-please," Nancy said with a tremulous voice. "Don't shoot us!"

"You should have thought of that before!" Roy rasped.

"Yeah," Taryn agreed uneasily.

"Well, at least let us have one last request. It's only human."

"Like—like what?" Taryn was getting rattled.

"I'm thirsty, Taryn. And I'm sure George is. Can we share that soda?"

Taryn hesitated.

"Let 'em," Roy ordered.

Taryn picked up the can. Nancy could see that her hands were quivering.

"Thanks." Nancy took the can. She held it out at arm's length. Behind Taryn, the moving form was getting closer. It *was* a boat.

She slipped her finger under the pop-top. She tilted the can toward Roy. . . .

She called his name, and when he turned to look an explosion of foam shot into his eyes.

"Aaaagh!" He jerked his arm across his face for protection, dropping his pistol over the side of the boat. Taryn spun toward him—and Nancy

213

pounced. Hurtling across the narrow boat, she knocked Taryn over the side. The gun flew out of her hands and into the water. As Nancy plunged into the Gulf with Taryn, she heard another splash behind her and knew George had followed.

"You—how—" Taryn sputtered helplessly, flailing her arms.

Nancy looked to her right. Two bright headlamps flicked on, aimed right at her. She waved. "Over here!"

The boat's motor revved up, then cut off. The bow came into view, and then three faces peering over it.

Ned, Frank, and Joe.

"A little late for a swim," Joe said. "I hear there are Portuguese men-of-war out here."

Ned reached down and pulled Nancy aboard. Frank and Joe helped George and Taryn.

Roy's cigarette boat took off at top speed.

Frank gave Taryn a sharp, level glance. "You, I think, have a lot of explaining to do," he said. He started the engine again. "And we have another rat to catch."

Nancy felt her body being forced backward into Ned's arms as Frank threw the engine into full throttle.

It was a terrific feeling.

Chapter
Twenty-Five

B<small>UCK</small> <small>WHOOPED</small> at the top of his lungs. He grabbed Mercedes around the waist and lifted her high into a dance step that defied gravity.

Nancy laughed. The party was perfect—a warm spring night on the old paddleboat, *Isabela Queen,* traveling slowly to nowhere along the Laguna Madre. "He's really back to his old self," she said to Ned, practically shouting to be heard over the music.

Ned danced closer to her. There was a broad smile on his face. "So are you!" he said.

The song ended, giving way to a slow ballad. Ned and Nancy walked back to the punch bowl and took two glasses. Then they went over to a nearby railing, where Frank was having a conversation with Bess and George. Joe stood next to them, listening to a Walkman.

"Can't resist hearing your name in the news, can you?" Nancy asked teasingly.

Joe smiled mischievously. "Actually, someone named Bess is getting most of the credit, for calling the police—"

"Yeah, Bess *Melvin,*" Bess said with a pout. "Can you believe it? My first shot at fame, and they can't even get my name right."

"Well, at least the police snapped into action," Ned said. "They must have notified the Coast Guard as soon as Bess called, because that cutter was right behind us."

"And they went after Roy like nobody's business," Joe added.

Frank nodded. "I think the pieces really fell together for them yesterday afternoon when Bruce's body was found washed up in Brownsville. They discovered the guy had a record for petty larceny, and they began to realize that maybe he was connected to this crime spree— maybe it was serious. So while we were tracking down Roy, they'd already begun their own investigation."

Nancy sighed. "I feel bad for Abe Quinones. I don't think Taryn was into this with all her heart."

"I think you're right," Frank said. "When they took the two of them in, Taryn was in tears. She said Roy had killed Bruce, rigged Buck's jet ski, stolen the Portuguese men-of-war, blown up our launch. Said she'd wanted to get out of it but was afraid Roy would kill her, too."

"Why did he try to kill Buck?" Bess asked. "No one believed he had found a body in that wreck."

"Roy didn't know it. He had just killed once, and his instant reaction to Buck's discovery was to kill Buck, too. He couldn't be reasoned with at that point," Frank explained.

"According to the news," Joe said, "Roy— alias a half-dozen other names—has a criminal record the length of his arm. He's been pulling scams since dropping out of high school at fifteen. It started with bogus mail-order offers. Over time he got braver and braver. For the last few years he's used phony papers to set up shops. He always managed to get the trust of someone prominent in town—usually female. Then slowly, systematically, he robbed people blind. As soon as the police started sniffing, he bolted."

"Someone like Taryn was perfect for him," Nancy added. "I can just see him listening to her sob stories about her father, working himself into a sympathetic rage—"

"Convincing her that taking money was the only way she would get back what was taken from her dad," George said.

Frank shrugged. "Well, she may get what she wanted, anyway. By the time she's sprung from the slammer her dad may be a multimillionaire from Ultralure."

"He and Rupert," Joe said dryly. "The dynamic duo."

Nancy's gaze wandered out onto the dance floor. Mercedes and Buck moved lazily to the music, wrapped tightly in each other's arms, interrupting their own rapturous stares with an occasional kiss. Dynamic duo. That's what they were, and it was about time they realized it. She sighed. That must be what being trapped on a desert island did to you. With a smile, she wondered if Ned could take her to that island.

A new song started playing—one of her favorites. George got up to dance with Joe. Bess got up to dance with whatever guy asked her, which was never a problem.

And at that moment Nancy felt herself being swept into an embrace. She looked up into Ned's eyes. "I don't think we should be standing still right now, do you?"

"Twist my arm, Nickerson."

Together they glided onto the dance floor.

Suddenly it seemed as if no one else was on the boat. Nancy hadn't felt so happy all week. Everything had finally fallen into place—Roy and Taryn were behind bars, Buck and Mercedes were back together, and the cutest guy on the *Isabela Queen* was still in love with her. Best of all, there were still three days before they had to go home.

Nancy smiled contentedly as she threw her arms around Ned. Who needed a desert island anyway?